Haunted Hearts

(ALL HALLOWS' EVE)

ELIZABETH ROSE

OLIVERHEBERBOOKS

Published by Oliver-Heber Books

0 9 8 7 6 5 4 3 2 1

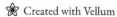 Created with Vellum

One

MEDIEVAL ENGLAND, 1300S

THE DARK LORD of Skull Manor watched her intently with haunting eyes, and Lady Lillith Bonnel found herself unable to look away.

Growing up together, Lord Blaze Payne, her family's neighbor, had always seemed to be able to read her mind. But today was different. Seeing him again after so long, even from across the graveyard, it felt as if he were able to look into her very soul.

"Lillith, turn around," whispered her mother, dabbing her tears with a hand cloth, taking a hold of Lillith's arm for support. Serena, Lillith's younger sister by two years, held on to her other arm. Her mother's handmaid, Posy, stood behind them, crying. A priest stood in front of the group of people from Alderwood Castle, praying over the coffin of her father that had just been lowered into the ground.

This all seemed like naught but a dream to Lillith. A nightmare, actually. She couldn't believe her father was really gone. Henri Bonnel had suffered from a bad heart that made him sweat and cough, sometimes having a hard time catching his breath. He'd turned to ale to ease his pain, and because of it was often well in his cups.

His mistake had been going out to hunt in his soused condition. That is what caused his demise. He'd gone riding at dusk and with only the page, Milo. Two went out, but only one returned.

Lillith had been told he'd been riding recklessly and ended up falling off his horse and onto his own blade.

Everything seemed to be happening so quickly. Her father's brother, Arthur was at the castle at the time, and insisted Henri be buried right away. Sadly, Lillith and Serena had been visiting the Baron Edward Bancroft, and had never even had the chance to say their final goodbyes to the man who'd sired them.

Their feuding neighbor from Skull Manor, Lord Blaze Payne, hadn't been invited to this grief-filled gathering, yet here he was, acting as if he belonged. The man had such gall to show up during this trying time in Lillith's life. Blaze watched every movement from a short distance away, not saying a word. He was not unlike his pet raven that lurked from the branch of a dead tree overhead, acting like it was looking for carrion.

Earlier, Lillith swore she saw a slight smirk lift up the corners of Blaze's mouth. Was he laughing at them and their misfortune? Had the feud between their families turn Blaze into a cold and cruel man through the years? He looked so arrogant as he leaned against the headstone of his own father's grave. It was almost as if he were silently saying her father had suffered the same fate now as his, and that he deserved it.

Blaze's father, Sir Roger Payne had died just last week of complications from an old wound he received in battle while fighting for the King years ago. Or at least that is what Lillith heard from the alewives and their wagging tongues.

Both Lillith and Blaze's fathers had been knights and lords who fought on the same side, for the English King Edward III. Those battles were justified, she supposed. But a part of her still wondered if the feud between their families that had lasted for five years now, should ever have happened at all.

Lillith's heart sped up just seeing Blaze this close, since she'd been forbidden to speak to him or even to ride past his manor ever since the feud began. She was told he and his family were witches and very dangerous indeed.

Dark clouds filled the sky as a storm brewed, quickly approaching and blocking the warm rays of the sun. The wind picked up, causing a rustling noise as dried leaves scurried across the ground like souls from the graveyard trying to escape their destined fate.

It was getting very close to All Hallows' Eve, the holiday that frightened Lillith. Being in a graveyard around this time of year was not where she wanted to be. It was said that the veil between the land of the living and dead was at its thinnest at this time of year. On All Hallows' Eve, supposedly dead souls could pierce that veil and rejoin those in the land of the living for a short time.

A shiver ran through Lillith's body. She wasn't sure if it was from the cool autumn air nipping at her nose, the stories of the dead coming back to life, or from the fact that Blaze had been staring at her ever since she arrived at the graveyard. It made her jittery, anxious, and on edge.

Ever since the feud began five years ago, Lillith had been hearing that Blaze was a witch - or warlock as the men of their craft were called. His mother was said to be a witch who even practiced dark magic. Lillith's father had believed the stories and convinced most in his family these stories were true as well. It is what started the wretched feud between them.

Henri Bonnel blamed Blaze's mother, Minerva for cursing Lillith's brother, Robert. One day he just disappeared. It was said he went mad and jumped from a cliff to his death. Witnesses swore they saw him, but Lillith's family never recovered his body, only his hat, which they found floating in the sea. Her father was certain Robert's body was taken by the forces of evil.

Robert's death had been foretold by Minerva, Blaze's mother, just hours before he disappeared. Lillith didn't want to believe all the awful stories, because she'd been good friends with Blaze growing up, and never thought of his family as wicked or dark.

Then again, her strong infatuation with Blaze might have made her miss the blatant truth.

Not able to help herself from looking at Blaze again, Lillith peeked back once more. This time, he nodded at her, causing her to gasp. Lillith's heart jumped and her head snapped back around to stare at her father's coffin. She needed to stay focused. If Blaze truly was a warlock like everyone said, he might be controlling her mind. She couldn't let him do that. As hard as she tried to think about nothing but her father, thoughts of her past filtered back into her mind of her time growing up with Blaze.

They were best friends at one time, going on explorations in the woods together, or horseback riding down to the river where they'd walk barefoot in the creek and skip rocks across the water. They'd also spent lots of time up on the hill where the Paynes' livestock grazed. Lillith would pick wildflowers and watch clouds, while Blaze practiced with his sword, always wanting to be a knight like his father. Blaze was always either at her home of Alderwood Castle, or she was at his, at Skull Manor. Those were happier times when life was simple and her only worry was if Blaze was going to try to kiss her or not.

They had kissed. Once. It was on her fifteenth birthday. It was only one little kiss, but it had made her feel special, excited, and extremely hopeful. She had wanted more than just a friendship with Blaze someday. She had wanted to become his wife. But now that she knew he was a warlock, those dreams changed.

Her head turned once more to see Blaze, her odd obsession with him like a moth to a flame. The moth knew it was going to its death, but couldn't stop itself from approaching the flame. Why couldn't she stop looking?

Was he really a warlock and his mother a witch? It made her truly wonder. And did his mother curse and kill her brother, Robert? If so, she wanted nothing to do with them and hoped the Paynes all rotted in hell. Lillith purposely glared at him this time, wanting Blaze to know that things could never be the same between them. Not after he'd lied to her and kept such dark secrets to himself.

The hostility that started growing within her quickly flew from her mind once his cloak opened in the breeze and she got a better look at his body. Blaze had always been a handsome boy, but in the past five years he seemed to have turned into a full-fledged, desirable man. Being three years older than Lillith's age of twenty, Blaze was now the same build and height of most of her father's knights.

Lillith watched from the corners of her eyes as he stretched out one arm over the top of the tall gravestone, showing little to no emotion at the death of her father. That made her wonder if he'd even shed a tear when his own father passed away. Emotions were never abundant with Blaze. He was always in control with every aspect of his life, never becoming the least bit unsettled no matter what happened. Had he even been affected by this horrific feud? Had he missed her at all? Sadly, she would never know the answers to those questions now.

Blaze slowly slid his arm off the gravestone and crossed his arms over his chest, fully aware that she was watching him, but too proud to look away. That made her wonder why he had even come to the funeral at all.

The dark lord's pet raven swooped down to settle itself on top of the head stone of Blaze's father, watching her with eyes just as dark and dangerous as its master. Pagans couldn't be buried on consecrated ground. However, it seemed Blaze convinced someone that his father was Catholic. Mayhap he was controlling minds after all.

Blaze's long black hair fell over his shoulders, lifting slightly in the late autumn breeze. His leather doublet clung to him, showing his lean body and broad chest. Through the opening at the top of his tunic, she noticed curls of crisp, dark hair.

Lillith felt a rush of heat run through her. Damn, why did he have to look so good? She didn't want to have these types of feelings for him. Not anymore. Not after what she'd learned about him and his family.

Why couldn't he be fat, bald, and ugly and covered with warts instead? Isn't that how all witches looked? It sure would make it easier for her to let him go if he had. Then again, what did it even matter? Things between them were over. Her father and his father might have had a verbal agreement that one day Blaze and Lillith would wed, but there was never anything put in writing.

At the beginning of the feud, her father changed his mind. Henri Bonnel had been securing a betrothal between Lillith and Baron Edward Bancroft before he died. Lillith and Serena just spent a sennight at the man's castle. The baron was rich, good-looking, and kind. Everything that made a good husband. Even if he wasn't Blaze.

Lillith wasn't in love with the baron, but what did it matter? After all, she would never marry a warlock! She was a devout Catholic, and wouldn't live in darkness the rest of her life, dooming her soul to hell for all eternity by becoming Blaze's wife.

"Sister, you need to throw a shovelful of dirt atop father's grave." Lillith's sister, Serena pushed the shovel into her hands, taking her attention now. "And stop staring at the warlock," she warned in a harsh whisper. Her eyes flashed over to Blaze and then back to Lillith again. "He's going to curse you, just like his mother did to Robert, if you don't stop it. We don't want you to die as well."

"Give me that," said Lillith under her breath, grabbing the shovel and scooping up some dirt. As sad as she was that her father and brother were gone, her anger overshadowed anything else at the moment.

How could Blaze never have told her he came from a family of witches? Lillith had been close to Blaze, and thought she'd known everything about him. They'd always been honest with each other. Or so she'd thought. He'd played her for a fool! His choice of deceiving her was unforgivable.

Lillith tossed the dirt into the hole and handed the shovel to the gravedigger. The sky above turned a shade darker. Thunder rumbled, echoing in the air. The cry of Blaze's raven almost seemed like an omen of death. When she looked back to Blaze once again, a bolt of lightning flashed in the sky directly above him, almost as if he'd summoned it. Or mayhap he was trying to strike down another of her family members with it, hoping to kill them too.

"It's starting to rain," called out one of the bystanders, causing the crowd to disperse.

"Get the women back to the castle, quickly," commanded Arthur. Her uncle, at least, had been here when her father died. Lillith had never really cared for the man since he'd always coveted everything her father had. Still, he was proving his worth she supposed, stepping in and helping to take care of things during this very difficult time.

"Sister, you're staring at him again," scolded Serena. "You're starting to scare me. Now please, stop it." Serena hooked her arm through Lillith's, trying to pull her in the opposite direction, but Lillith didn't budge. She continued to watch Blaze, wondering just what kind of man he really was now. "People are going to talk and say you still have eyes for the dark lord of Skull Manor if you keep that up."

"I promise you, I don't like him anymore," Lillith said, shaking her head slowly.

God's eyes, her father's death would change everything for Lillith now. He'd been in the process of drawing up the papers to betroth her to Baron Bancroft, one of the richest and most eligible men in England. Her life had been about to change for the better, but now, she didn't know where she stood. She was already well past marrying age. If she waited any longer, she'd end up stuck with an old, fat widower if she was even that lucky. Lillith could only hope now that Uncle Arthur could carry out her father's dealings and still secure the betrothal for her with Sir Edward Bancroft. The sooner the better as far as she was concerned. Lillith couldn't wait to get far away from Alderwood Castle, the feud, and most of all, Lord Blaze Payne.

Almost as if Blaze could hear Lillith's thoughts, his head snapped up and his dark eyes interlocked with hers. Lillith gasped, her body tingling and stiffening, making her legs feel like wood. With his eyes locked on her, she couldn't even find the will to move or the breath to speak.

The wind picked up, blowing the tree limbs, causing their branches to sway and creak, threatening to break. The raven squawked from its perch, then flew over and landed on Blaze's shoulder. Slowly, the dark lord turned and headed back to his horse that was neighing and pawing the ground in anticipation of the storm. The man's long, black cloak billowed out behind him in the breeze, making him look like a warlock if she'd ever seen one – which she hadn't. Still, it was how she expected one to look.

"Enough! Let's go, Lillith." Serena took her hand and ran back to the wagon, pulling Lillith along with her as the sky opened up and the rain pelted down drenching them all.

"Someday they will pay for what they did to Robert," Lillith gave her promise to her sister as she climbed into the wagon. Another chill swept through her. When Lillith looked back to the spot Blaze had been, the dark lord was gone.

* * *

Lord Blaze Payne made it back to Skull Manor and entered his courtyard riding in the pouring rain. Sliding off his horse, he handed the reins to his stablemaster, Orvyn. His pet raven, Ebony, flew up to the roof to find shelter under one of the overhangs.

"My lord, I need to speak with you," said Orvyn, taking the reins and looking up at him, using his hand to shelter his face from the rain. Orvyn was old and slow, and always wanted to talk. The man's wet clothes clung to his overweight body, reminding Blaze of his mother's fat cat the last time it fell into the watering trough. Blaze wasn't much for small talk, and rather liked his solitude. He also didn't have time for this right now.

"We'll talk later, Orvyn. Just tend to my horse for now, and make sure to rub her down," he called back over his shoulder as he hurried across the courtyard and up the stairs to the keep. He nodded a greeting to some of his men in the great hall, not stopping, but rather walking right past them. Blaze headed down the corridor to his solar, wanting to be alone.

Seeing Lady Lillith and her family at the cemetery today upset him greatly. Because of the ongoing feud, he hadn't spoken to her and had only seen her from a distance in five long years now. This wasn't the way things were supposed to be. Blaze used to be the one to protect Lillith when they were children. He'd learned to use a sword at an early age, and had always brought it with them when they'd climbed the hill to see the sheep and watch clouds. He had felt like a knight protecting his lady whenever they rode into the forest to explore and look for mushrooms so Lillith could make him his favorite soup.

Aye, Blaze lost his heart to the enticing girl long ago, and would never forget her. In his mind, he thought that Lilly would be the one he'd marry someday although no betrothal had ever been formally made. Still, he'd had no doubt that they'd always be together. Lillith used to run straight to him when something was troubling her. He'd always been able to calm her with just a hug and a wide smile. But that was before they became mortal enemies. Before the damned feud.

Today, the wench glared at him as if she wanted to kill him. Blaze didn't like the feeling at all. Their families had been feuding for so long now, that it was getting hard to even remember what they were truly fighting about.

Blaze threw open the door to his solar, stepped over the threshold, and stopped short, letting loose with a low groan when he saw his mother. Now he remembered the reason for the feud. His mother, the witch, had been accused of cursing Lillith's brother, causing him to go mad and jump from a cliff to his death.

The last thing he needed right now was seeing his mother, Lady Minerva, here at the manor. Finding her in his private solar only added to his frustration. He hadn't seen his mother in years now, and wasn't in a hurry to do so again. Wherever the woman went, trouble seemed to follow.

"Nay," he mumbled, shaking his head, thinking this was the last thing he wanted to deal with tonight. It was because of her that the family feud started in the first place. His mother didn't know discretion. Because of it, she had ruined Blaze's life and almost caused his father to lose everything, including the manor and even his title of knight.

Minerva looked up at him, not seeming at all surprised to see him, although it took him aback that she was here at all. Her fat black cat, her familiar, sat right atop his table. One lone candle burned brightly from an iron holder on the table, lighting up each wrinkle and subtle crease on his mother's face. Five years had aged the woman more than he had imagined.

Her black hair was pulled back tight and twisted into a knot. Newfound streaks of gray ran through it. But even having aged, she still looked impeccable, he had to admit. Her gown was crisp and fresh and not wrinkled at all. She was clean, and the scent of rosewater drifted from her hair. Minerva wore colored gemstone rings of red and purple on her long, tapered fingers. The stones glittered in the candlelight, making her look like an elegant lady instead of a damned witch. Blaze noticed her crystal pendant resting against her chest, hanging from a silver chain around her neck. She used it as a pendulum for getting answers to questions. She'd let Blaze try it a few times, but he never could seem to make it work.

Minerva sat with her back straight and her chin jutting out, acting as if she belonged here, but Blaze didn't agree. Her presence at the manor made Blaze extremely uncomfortable. Skull Manor was under his command now, since the death of his father a sennight ago. As far as he was concerned, she wasn't coming back here to live. He wouldn't allow it. She'd left of her own accord but wouldn't be welcomed back with open arms. His gaze slowly slid down to the table and he let out a deep sigh.

He supposed he shouldn't have been surprised to see her fortune-telling cards spread out in an arc in front of her. Half the cards were turned over, and the other half were yet uncovered. Just like his life right now – unpredictable, unseen, and unsure.

Blaze never liked his mother's cards. As a child they used to terrify him since his mother often very accurately predicted deaths. Even as a grown man now, Blaze still felt cautious around the blasted things. Every time his mother pulled the deck out of her little black velvet bag that hung at her side, something chaotic, life-threatening, or unwelcome seemed to transpire. He was sure tonight would be no different.

"Mother, why are you here?" he asked in a low voice, his fists clenching and his body filling with frustration.

Her eyes opened wide and then her thin brows dipped, making the creases in her forehead more prevalent. "Is that any way to greet your mother? We haven't seen each other in five years, Blaze."

Blaze sighed and closed the door. "I suppose you heard about Father's death and that is why you're here?"

"I know about it, but not from you. It would have been nice if you'd told me," she spat. "I saw his death in the cards and came at once."

At one time, Blaze knew exactly what his life held in store. He'd been following in his father's footsteps, training to be a knight. Unfortunately, it never happened. Because of his mother, everything in his life turned for the worse. No one wanted the son of a witch in their service. He'd been called a warlock behind his back, and that didn't sit right with him at all.

His father had even been shunned by his liege, the Earl of Birmingham, once he'd heard the rumors that Minerva was a witch. Actually, they weren't rumors, although his father had denied the fact. There had been a horrible argument between Minerva and Roger because of the threat to Roger's title, position, and everything he owned. That's when his mother left, not saying where she was going, and barely even bidding him a farewell.

These past five years had been hell for Blaze. He had been helping his father convince everyone that nothing was amiss with their family. The earl had eventually welcomed Roger Payne back as one of his knights, but hadn't continued with Blaze's training. Instead, Earl Birmingham kept promising to finish what they'd started soon, but it never happened. It was no secret that the earl believed the rumors. Even though his father had been welcomed back, the earl never accepted Blaze.

Even though Blaze was lord of the manor now, it was a courtesy title only. Without being knighted, no one would ever really respect him. What scant amount of knights there had been at Skull Manor, left as soon as Blaze's father died. Everyone was wary of Blaze. He supposed it was because he looked like a warlock with his stark features and long black hair. His father had been fair-skinned and blond with blue eyes. Blaze, unfortunately took on the features of his mother with black hair and eyes almost as dark as coal. Why, in God's name, did Minerva have to return?

"I didn't know where you went, Mother, so how could I have contacted you?" asked Blaze with an edge to his voice. His relationship with his father had been a strong one. He and his mother had never seen eye-to-eye on anything.

"Your father knew I was in France staying with my sister," she said.

"Well, he never told me."

"Hrmph," she scoffed. "I'm not surprised. Roger was adamant not to let your life be affected by my ways and beliefs. That's why he sent me away and forbade me to ever return, once the feud started."

"He is the one who sent you away?" This surprised Blaze since his father had made it sound the opposite way around. "I don't believe it. How could you just leave and not return or even contact us in five long years?"

"Yes, time did go fast," she said with little emotion. "You know, I always planned on returning," she said nonchalantly. "I figured I'd give it some time and then I'd come back and tell you anything you wanted to know. I was sure that after a while everyone would forget about what happened. That would give you time to be knighted and to marry and start a family." She turned her head to look at him directly. "My cards tell me that none of these things have happened yet. Am I right?"

"If you would just ask me and talk to me instead of consulting those damned cards, I would have told you as much."

"Would you have, really?"

"What difference does it make?" he said, clenching his jaw. "I'm sure you would have heard it from all the wagging tongues around here eventually."

"Blaze, I'd like to go to the graveyard to pay my last respects to your father," she told him. "I don't like it that he died so soon, before we had a chance to make amends."

"You had five long years to make amends," he grumbled. "Besides, you can't go to the graveyard." He walked closer to the table and her stupid cat actually hissed at him. "Lord Henri Bonnel just died and his family will be frequenting his gravesite. I don't want you there."

"You sound embarrassed of me. Is this true?"

The room remained dark except for the flicker of the flame that cast jumping shadows on the stone walls of his solar. There was no fire on the hearth, and the air was as cold as a tomb. To make matters worse, the only light in the room was from a black candle made of beeswax stuck into a tall metal candleholder.

Black. It wasn't a good color for anything as far as Blaze was concerned. Or, at least not after one was accused of being a witch or warlock. All he needed was someone to find black candles in his solar, and they'd be pointing fingers at him and calling him a warlock once again. He had hoped that was all behind him now. It had almost seemed to be. But now his father was dead and his mother was back home. One problem ended and another began.

"Mother, how can you even ask me that question?" he ground out, trying his best to keep his temper in check. "Your witchy ways need to stop. It is ruining our lives. You need to become more discreet before you get us burned at the stake. What in the name of the devil are you thinking? That you can amble back into my life after so long and pick up right where you left off? It doesn't work that way. How did you even get into my solar in the first place without being seen?"

"Who said I wasn't seen?" She looked up and flashed a sardonic smile.

"Damn it, please don't tell me my entire household saw you strolling back in here with your bag of tricks over your shoulder?" He began to pace the room, running a weary hand through his long hair.

"Don't worry, it wasn't your entire household." She studied the cards and didn't bother to look up at him when she spoke. Nothing ever seemed to shake her. She either had nerves of steel, or the woman was totally heartless. He decided it was a little of each.

"What do you mean not my entire household?" He didn't like the sound of this, and already regretted asking. Still, he needed to know.

"Just that man at the stable saw me, that's all."

"Stable? Who? What was this man's name?" Blaze stopped pacing and held his breath, waiting for her answer.

"I don't remember his name. He was about my age and slightly overweight. His hair was balding right here," she said, tapping the back of her head. "He wasn't here when I lived at Skull Manor, so I am guessing your father hired him since I left. The man is pesky and likes to talk a lot. I mean, after all, I only asked him to care for my horse, but he wanted to know everything about me."

"God's toes, nay. Not Orvyn." If anyone had to have seen her, why did it have to be him? Lightning flashed outside the open window and thunder rumbled the walls, imitating his dark mood.

"Orvyn . . . Orvyn." She looked up in the air and tapped a long finger against her lips. "Yes, I think that was his name. You see, I wasn't really listening to him as he went on and on about some knight or lady, or whatever it was he chattered about." She reached out and flipped over a card, still clutching the rest of the deck in one hand.

"Hellfire and damnation, if Orvyn knows you're here, it's no different than shouting it from the battlements. Your arrival is no longer a secret." Blaze started pacing again.

"It shouldn't need to be a secret. I live here," said his mother. "Blaze, are you saying your stablemaster has a wagging tongue?"

"That's putting it mildly." Blaze forced a laugh. "I didn't even want him here at all, but we had to take him in since he was sent here by the earl. You see, I am trying my best to make amends with Earl Birmingham."

"Oh, so you still want to be a knight."

"Of course, I do. Why wouldn't I? It's what every nobleman wants."

"You don't need to wait for the earl's approval. Go offer your services somewhere else. You can always earn a living hiring out your sword. After all, you are good with a blade."

Blaze had considered that, but it wasn't an honorable job at all. It would stop him from ever becoming a knight. He also didn't want to leave Skull Manor. Down deep, he really didn't want to be far away from Lillith. A part of him kept hope alive that they could still be together someday.

"My reputation proceeds me now," he told his mother. "If I can't convince Earl Birmingham that I'm not a warlock, no one else will believe me."

"Oh, well, who even cares about being a knight?" she asked. "You're a warlock, Blaze. If you spent more time embracing your craft instead of playing with swords, things might go better for you."

"There is no way in hell embracing being a warlock is better than being a knight. Neither is it something I'd ever consider doing. I don't practice your pagan ways. I'm a Catholic now, like father."

"Hmph," she snorted. "If you knew the first thing about our ways, you would have embraced them instead. I never could convert your father, no matter how hard I tried. However, I must say, I respect that once he discovered my secret, he never breathed a word of it to anyone."

"Is that why I'm an only child, Mother? Father didn't find out you were a witch until after I was born, did he? I'll bet he never would have married you if you'd been honest with him from the start."

"What difference does it make?" she asked. "We had some good times together, but now it's over. Even if he's gone, at least I have you, Blaze."

Like that was supposed to make him feel better?

"You can't stay here, Mother. I won't let you," he said curtly, not wanting to hold in his frustration any longer.

"What?" She turned to him, looking shocked. "Son, this is my home."

"Not anymore, it's not. And please, don't force me to kick you out, because you know I will if I have to. However, you are still my mother and I'd rather you just left on your own."

"Oh, stop all your fussing, Blaze." His mother flipped over another card. "You realize that all your worrying about things that don't really matter is going to make you age quickly."

Blaze couldn't believe his mother's attitude at all. No wonder his father threw her out on her ear. "I worked hard these past years, trying to erase from people's minds the things they thought about me when you were careless enough to be discovered. You being here is only going to make matters worse."

"I did nothing wrong. It's not my fault that boy died. I only sent a missive to Lord Bonnel to warn him to keep his son off cliffs when I saw in the cards that Robert was in grave danger."

"The tower card?" he asked curiously, knowing that one well. It was a tower being struck by lightning and two people falling from it, head first.

"Yes, that's the one. Followed by the death card. See? It was evident it was going to happen. I had to warn his parents."

"No, you didn't. And you didn't need to tell them you saw all this by reading fortune-telling cards. What the hell is the matter with you?"

"I thought if they knew the source, they'd believe me. And thank me later."

"And we see how well that plan worked!"

"I only did it for you, Blaze. You and Lillith. I didn't want the girl you were sweet on to lose her brother, and so I warned them."

"You must have frightened poor Robert out of his mind. That is probably why it is said he was delirious and jumped from a cliff in a storm."

"Nonsense. I did no such thing. I did not curse that boy, I assure you."

"That's not what the Bonnels think."

"They overreact," she said, swiping a hand through the air. "I had good intentions to help them, but they turned everything around."

"Your actions started a feud between our families. A feud that has never ended."

"Really?" She looked up in curiosity. "Oh, that old goat, Henri Bonnel, was always looking for a fight. It was bound to happen sooner or later."

"Mother, there was never trouble between our families before that."

"Things happen," she said with a shrug. "We are all forced to make changes if we're going to survive."

"If it wasn't for you, I'd be a knight right now and I'd also be married to Lilly."

Her head snapped up and a smile crossed her face. "So that's why you're not married yet. You're waiting for the Bonnel girl.

Well, it's never going to happen, Blaze. I'm sure by now she holds her father's beliefs about us. She'll never change, and you won't be able to convince her of anything different."

"Our fathers both died without ever resolving the feud. I don't want to go to my grave with Lilly glaring at me in hate, the way she did today."

"Oh. So, you saw her today then?"

"Aye," he admitted. "I went to the graveyard when they were burying her father."

"I wouldn't worry about things, Blaze. Things will turn out just the way they're supposed to."

"Is that something you saw in your damned cards?" he asked snidely. "Because, the death of Lord Bonnel is something we should be very concerned with."

"Whatever for?" She shrugged her shoulders. "I wasn't even here so they can't blame his death on me this time."

"Mayhap not, but something tells me that this time they're going to blame it all on me."

Two

"THEY'LL BLAME YOU? Bid the devil, Blaze, what did you do?" asked Minerva.

"I did nothing," he told her. "However, I did happen to come across Henri Bonnel's dead body on the road, and I think his pageboy might have seen me bending over the man's body."

"What difference does it make if he saw you? You didn't kill the man. Did you?"

"Nay, of course not. I believe Henri was soused and fell off his horse and onto his own blade. Or, at least that is what it looked like."

"Well, what did the Bonnels say about it when you brought the body back to Alderwood Castle?"

"I . . . didn't."

"What do you mean you didn't?" Her eyebrows dipped. "You just said you were there."

"Aye, I was. But I decided it would do no good if I got involved."

"So you left him there?"

"I knew the boy was going back to the castle for help. I was wearing my cloak with my hood covering my head so I don't think the boy recognized me. However, when I heard him approaching, I moved so fast that I didn't realize it until later that I had dropped my hunting dagger."

"Oh, no. That's not good."

"I'm pretty sure he saw the dagger on the ground next to the dead body. I had just killed a rabbit and there was blood on it. He was so frightened that he bolted away. I picked up my blade as soon as he left, but it might have been too late."

"And you didn't help Lord Bonnel?"

"He was dead, Mother! I checked his pulse. There was nothing I could do. Staying there was only going to raise suspicion and make more trouble for me. He died by a blade to the gut. It was his own fault."

"His dagger was still there, then?"

"Of course it was. However, it looked like before he died he managed to pull it out. Don't you see? Because I was there and had a bloody dagger, rumors will surface that I killed him and removed my blade before anyone could find out."

"Yes. They would say something like that, wouldn't they?" she said in thought.

"I can only hope the boy didn't recognize me."

"Which dagger were you using, Blaze?"

"The one you gave me with the moons and stars and skull on the hilt."

"That's not good," she said, seeming concerned, shaking her head. "That one is too recognizable. It would be best if you put that blade away for a while and used a different one for now," suggested his mother.

"Don't worry. I already did."

Hot wax pooled on the wooden table around the candle holder telling Blaze that his mother had been here for quite some time. Damn. How had he not known of her arrival? If he had been at the manor instead of at the graveyard, mayhap he could have stopped her from ever stepping foot inside his home. Too late now. His mother was here, and with her arrival, bad things were already happening. There was no doubt in his mind that a whirlwind of chaos was about to follow.

"Well, I certainly won't leave you now, Blaze. If you're in trouble, you'll need me." She narrowed her eyes and spoke softly. "Are you sure you didn't kill Henri Bonnel? After all, the man was mean and quite quarrelsome. I can't say I'll miss him."

"Nay! I told you, I had nothing to do with his death. I'm sure it was just an accident. He was always riding fast and hunting while drinking. It finally caught up to him, I guess." Blaze paced to the other side of the room.

"Well, no matter what, we need to cleanse ourselves of all this negativity." Minerva reached over and fanned at the air with her hand. A swirl of smoke rose up from burning herbs that were twisted together making a wand, resting on his favorite silver dish. The smoke filled the room with an odd aroma.

"Sage," Blaze complained, knowing the scent only too well. "Mother, I hate the smell of sage and you know it." He stormed across the room, ripping the wand off his favorite plate, throwing the burning herbs to the floor and stomping out the smoldering stalks with his foot.

Her cat, Sam, was spooked and jumped off the table and hid somewhere in the room.

"You should leave that alone, Blaze. It's taking the negativity out of the room." She picked up a bowl of salt, pinching a few granules in her fingers and tossing them at him.

"Stop that nonsense," he growled, holding up his hand to cover his face.

Minerva purposely took a deep breath and released it slowly. "Believe me, there are some hostile vibrations in the air right now." Her head turned and her eyes focused on the smashed herbs under his boot.

"I can think of a much better way to remove negativity," he scowled, already wondering if he'd made a bad choice by not kicking the woman out of here by now. He brushed the ashes away and continued to wipe off the plate with his sleeve.

"You sound as if you're upset, son. Why?"

"Did your cards tell you that or was it just obvious?" He walked over and placed the etched silver plate back atop the mantle, fixing it in precisely the right place.

"Why do you even care about that stupid plate?" asked his mother.

"It was a gift that the earl gave Father when he made him his head knight," he explained. "I am hoping it'll bring me good luck." Blaze bent down and lit a fire on the hearth.

"Luck doesn't just happen, it's something we create," she told him. "If you have ill luck, it is no one's fault but your own."

"Stop it." He got up and spun around in anger, holding the iron poker out, pointing to her with it. The candle on the table blew out from the breeze coming in the window, and several of the Tarot cards fluttered to the floor.

"I see you're still not accepting who and what you really are," said his mother, bending over and picking up the cards.

"I wish you wouldn't say things like that."

"Why not?"

"Because, I'm not a warlock. I have no powers. Neither do you." He turned and shoved the poker back into the holder on the hearth.

"We get our power from nature and things of the earth. I can show you how, son."

"Nay. I don't care about that. I am not like you. I take after Father."

"Our only limitations in life are the ones we bestow upon ourselves. Now, stop speaking like this, because you're only going to attract more challenges into your life."

"I hope not, because enough bad things have been happening around here lately."

"Well, whether something is bad or good is only an opinion. Just remember that."

Blaze was getting tired of his mother spouting words of wisdom. "I don't think Lord Bonnel's family would agree with that, since they've lost two family members in the past five years."

"No, of course they wouldn't." She pointed at three cards on the table. "Look at these cards, Blaze."

"What about them?"

"The emperor card depicts you." Curiosity got the best of him and he walked over to take a look.

"What's that?" he asked, pointing to the nine of swords. It was a picture of a man in bed, covering his face. Nine swords pointed directly at him.

"That card shows you're worried, anxious, and extremely concerned about something. Something that you don't think will end well."

"Oh, you mean because the last card is death?" asked Blaze, eyeing the card of a skeleton riding a horse, sorry now that he even looked at the card reading at all. "Why are you even showing me this? Just to make me see that life no longer has anything to offer?"

"Not at all. I'm showing you, because we can figure out how to fix your life, once we know what is causing the energy from flowing freely."

"Hah! I'd like to see you fix that," he spat, pointing at the card of death.

"The death card doesn't always mean physical death," she assured him. "Sometimes, it means the death of a habit, or a new change of life altogether."

"I hope you're right, Mother," said Blaze, not liking any of this and having a bad feeling about it all. "I hope you're right."

* * *

"Uncle Arthur, thank you for staying and helping us through these hard times." Lillith sat at the dais at Alderwood Castle during the meal that followed her father's funeral. She was still devastated by his passing and also shaken because of seeing Blaze today. Her stomach twisted into a huge knot. She had no desire to eat. Instead, she used her spoon to push her food around her trencher, stuck in her thoughts of the past.

"My pleasure," said Arthur, sitting in her father's chair, next to her mother who was still weeping and dabbing at her eyes. Serena sat next to Lillith, not seeming very hungry either. The storm had started to let up outside, thankfully. The occupants in the great hall remained in a quiet and sullen mood over the death of their lord. "After all, Henri was my brother and it's the least I can do," continued Arthur.

Out of six boys, Arthur was the only Bonnel brother still alive. All the rest had died over the years in battles or accidents of one kind or another.

"My lord, the horses as well as the livestock are all secured now, should the storm continue," said one of the guards, walking to the front of the dais and bowing his head.

"Good, good," said Arthur, picking up his cup and taking a sip of wine. "Ask the steward to bring the tally books to my solar immediately so I can go over them as soon as the meal is finished."

"Aye, my lord."

"Thank you, that'll be all."

"Uncle, do you really think that is necessary right now?" asked Lillith. "Before the estate is tended to, we need to properly let everyone mourn my father's passing."

"Yes, Arthur. Lillith is right," agreed her mother, Beatrice. "We need to take time to mourn our loss."

"Excuse me, my lord, but the undertaker still needs to be paid for your brother's burial," said Sir Barnaby, the steward of the castle.

Huntley, the undertaker, was also the castle's carpenter. He was the one who made the wooden coffins. Huntley also prepared the dead bodies for burial from all the surrounding areas.

"Ah, yes, I suppose so." Arthur's hand went to his waist but then he shook his head. "I don't seem to have my money pouch on me. He'll just have to wait until the morrow to get paid."

"But he is at the graveyard now, awaiting his payment," said Barnaby. "Shall I send a page with your message?"

Arthur snorted, focusing on his food. "Nay, don't bother. If he wants to be a fool and wait out in the rain, then let him. He'll figure it out eventually. I am eating my meal now and won't be disturbed. As I said, he can wait."

"Aye, my lord," said the steward, looking concerned, and heading away from the table.

"Serena," Lillith whispered to her sister. "It's not right to make the undertaker wait in the rain for his fee when Uncle Arthur has no intention of paying him until the morrow."

"I agree," said Serena with a nod. "Father would never have agreed to such a thing. He always saw to matters anon and didn't like unfinished deals."

"He's probably turning in his grave right now," said Lillith. "Father never did agree with the way Arthur handles things." Arthur was often impetuous, acting too fast and not thinking things through before acting.

"Huntley should at least be told that no one is coming," whispered Serena.

"I agree. I'll go to the graveyard and pay him myself." Lillith got up from her seat. "Don't tell Uncle or he'll forbid me to leave."

"Lillith, where are you going?" asked Arthur, looking up and then taking a big bite of bread. "Your mother told me that you are concerned about your upcoming betrothal and I wanted to talk to you about it." He chewed and spoke at the same time. "After all, I'll be assuming my brother's position as head of the family now, as well as claiming everything that was his."

"You're taking Father's place?" Lillith's eyes shot over to her sister. Serena looked just as surprised as she felt. "Father only died last night and already you are claiming his title, his castle, and his land? Can you even do that?"

"He can, daughter," answered her mother with a sniffle. "Arthur is the last of the Bonnel brothers. Since Henri's heir was Robert and he is dead, everything will pass to Arthur now."

"Including his wife," said Arthur with a smile, placing his hand over Beatrice's. Lust already leaked from his dark eyes.

"What?" gasped Lillith and Serena together.

"Mother, is this true?" asked Serena. "Are you going to marry Uncle Arthur?"

"I – I suppose so," said Beatrice, pulling her hand back slowly. "I'm a widow now and need a husband. Plus, I don't want to leave Alderwood. Your father had it set up in writing that if anything ever happened to him, Arthur would take his place. That included being my husband, and also father to you girls, if Arthur wasn't already married."

Arthur had never married, and Lillith believed it was because the man didn't have much to offer. That is, not until now.

"Lillith, Henri and I were talking about your betrothal just before he left on the hunt. He hadn't had the chance to tell you yet, but a missive arrived before you and Serena even got home," said Arthur, taking a big bite of a chicken leg.

"What kind of missive?" asked Lillith curiously.

Arthur took a swig of ale to wash down the food and then answered her. "It was from Baron Edward Bancroft. He has agreed to your betrothal."

"He has?" This surprised Lillith, since it was the first she had heard about it. The baron didn't bother to even tell her, and she was just there visiting at his castle.

"Lillith, it seems your little trip with Serena to meet him is what sealed the deal," added her mother. "He wrote in the missive that he enjoyed having both of you there. He called you both charming women."

"Oh, sister, that is good news," said Serena, looking up at her with a smile.

"Yes, Lillith, it is," said her mother. "You'll be marrying a wealthy man and will never need for anything in your life."

I – I suppose so," said Lillith, flashing a smile. She had truly wanted this betrothal ever since she heard Blaze was a warlock and the feud began. But now, after seeing him today, old feelings were stirred and rising to the surface again. She felt confused and her head became fuzzy. Mayhap she didn't really want this betrothal with the baron as much as she thought she had after all.

"The baron has already started posting the wedding banns," announced Arthur. "As soon as we can agree on arrangements and a dowry, we'll have the wedding."

This announcement made Lillith feel suddenly trapped. For some reason, she felt as if she were betraying Blaze. There was absolutely nothing between them anymore, so it didn't matter. Yet, part of her felt like it did.

"If you'll excuse me, I am not feeling well." Lillith hurried away from the table without waiting for approval, making her way out to the courtyard. Everything was happening too fast. She didn't know what to think. The rain had let up as quickly as it came, so it would make her trip to the graveyard to pay the under-taker easier. Lillith decided that mayhap a ride in the fresh air would help to clear her head.

It didn't take long to get to the cemetery and find Huntley. He was standing near her father's grave. The gravediggers were just finishing up filling in the hole since they'd waited until the storm let up to complete it.

"Huntley, there you are," she said, stopping her horse. The man ran over to take the reins as she dismounted.

"Lady Lillith? What are you doing here? I expected to see a messenger, not you. Are you here unescorted?" Huntley didn't live at Alderwood Castle, but instead, in a small cottage in the village between her castle and Lord Blaze's manor. He worked as an undertaker for both sides.

"My uncle can be hard-headed at times," she explained. "I wanted to make sure you and the grave diggers were paid as is proper." Lillith opened her pouch and removed three coins, handing them to Huntley. The gravediggers wandered over to collect their share. Huntley gave them each a coin and then stuck the last one in his pocket.

"Thank you, my lady. You have always been kind to me as well as everyone in the village." Huntley bowed slightly.

"I appreciate you taking care of my father's burial so quickly. However, I wish I could have seen him before the coffin was closed and nailed shut."

"I'm sorry, my lady. I wanted to wait until you and Lady Serena returned from your trip, but Lord Arthur insisted on taking care of things right away. He said it would be easier for your mother that way since she was so distraught."

"Aye, I suppose he's right. Well, thank you, Huntley. I'll be off then." She was about to mount her horse, but Huntley stopped her.

"My lady, there is something I feel I need to mention."

"What is it?" she asked curiously.

He looked over at the gravediggers and waited until they climbed aboard the wagon and started away before he spoke.

"There is something about your father's death that bothers me. I know it's not my place to speak freely, but he was always good to me, and I feel you should know."

"Know what? What are you talking about?" The man's odd choice of words made her curious.

"Well, you know I really shouldn't say anything since I don't know all the facts. It's really just idle gossip."

"I see." She reached into her pouch and pulled out another coin and held it out to him. "You deserve more than the gravediggers. I'm sorry. I shouldn't have overlooked it."

"Nay. That's not what I mean." Huntley held up a hand and shook his head. "It's not money I'm after, my lady. All I want is to give you the information. I'm not sure if you know."

"Huntley, I don't understand. What are you trying to say?" Clutching the coin, she slowly lowered her hand, seeing how upset the man suddenly became. "Tell me what's bothering you."

"It's what Milo saw. Or thinks he saw."

"Go on," she said.

"A man was seen next to your father's dead body. He was bent over him and touching his face."

"What are you saying? Who was it?" she gasped. She had thought her father was alone, except for Milo who he left in the dust. By the time the page caught up to him, he was dead.

"Milo said the man he saw wore a hooded cloak. It was dusk so he didn't see his face and doesn't know his identity, but he thinks it could have been Lord Payne."

"Why didn't anyone mention this to me?"

"I don't know, my lady. All I know is that Lord Arthur thought it best not to upset your mother with too many details of her husband's death."

"That's preposterous. We need to know what was going on."

"I agree," said Huntley. "Especially after what the witch did to your brother."

This didn't sit right with Lillith. She had been doubting from the start that the Paynes had anything to do with Robert's death, but now she wasn't so sure. Huntley was insinuating her father's demise had something to do with the Paynes as well.

"Huntley, are you saying Lord Payne had something to do with my father's death?"

"I don't know, my lady. But talk is that the man Milo saw was Lord Blaze."

"You can't go around accusing innocent people of foul play with no proof."

"Well, Milo says he saw a witchy-looking dagger on the ground next to your father's body. There was blood on it. He was so frightened that he ran for help. When he returned with Lord Arthur, the dagger as well as the man were gone."

"Why would anyone purposely want to harm my father? Especially Lord Blaze. This is absurd." As soon as she said the words, she knew that it wasn't so hard to believe. After all, they'd been feuding with the Paynes and things had gotten out of hand at times. Now that Roger Payne, Blaze's father was gone, perhaps Blaze was carrying out the plan by himself.

"I'm sorry, my lady. You're right. I'm sure there is nothing to it at all. I didn't mean to speak so brashly."

"You only insinuated what everyone else is thinking." Lillith knew Huntley was being careful with his words because it was no secret how close Lillith and Blaze had been while growing up. Everyone knew it. They had been seen together by all. Lillith had even told all her hired help that someday she and Blaze would marry and become man and wife. Now, she was truly regretting her immature actions.

"Still, I was out of line, my lady."

"Did Milo get a good look at the blade?" she asked. "Is it recognizable in any way?"

"I don't know much more, my lady. Just that it had moons and stars on it and a skull on the hilt. I suggest you talk to the page to find out more."

"Yes, of course. I will." Lillith didn't need to talk to Milo, because she knew that blade was Blaze's. She'd seen him with it many times in the past.

"Thank you, my lady. I'll be going now." Huntley turned to go but Lillith stopped him.

"Huntley, thank you," she said, handing him the extra coin after all. "And please, for now, until I can find out more, do not tell anyone else what you told me."

"I won't." He pocketed the coin. "Thank you, my lady. Let me escort you back to your castle now. It's not safe in these woods alone."

"I'm sure I'll be fine, but I'll take you up on your offer since it looks like the storm is about to return and I don't have a torch to light my way."

"I'll also protect you from any witches or warlocks that we might encounter," he said, mounting his horse.

"I'm sure we'll see none of those," she scoffed, shivering when the thought of Blaze's intense stare went through her mind once more.

Three

BLAZE MADE his way out to the stables, wanting to figure out a way to try to keep Orvyn from telling everyone his mother had arrived and was living at Skull Manor once again. That alone was going to throw his household into chaos. After the death of Lillith's brother five years ago when his mother got careless with her discretion, everyone became on edge. The feud with the Bonnels was triggered, and things finally managed to calm down only after his mother left.

"Lord Payne, hello. What brings you out to the stable in this weather?" Orvyn walked out of a stall wiping his hands on a rag. "Of course, the rain has pretty much let up now so I suppose the weather isn't all that bad anymore. Will you be wanting your horse saddled to go for another ride then?"

"Nay," he answered with a shake of his head, meaning to get right to the point.

"Did I do something wrong, my lord? I hope you aren't upset with me. It's a reward just being in your presence. The earl sending me here was the best thing that ever happened to me."

Blaze was sure the earl was only trying to rid himself of this pest by sending him here, and Blaze couldn't blame him. If Blaze hadn't been trying to get back in the earl's good graces, he'd send

Orvyn away as well. However, if he ever wanted to be accepted anywhere as a knight, he couldn't be even remotely rebellious in the least. Just listening

to the man ramble on and on made Blaze feel exhausted. "You stabled the horse of . . . of a lady a little while ago," he said, not wanting to say who it was in case the man hadn't really realized who Minerva was.

"Oh, your mother? Aye. What a fine lady she is."

"Yes. My mother," he said, closing his eyes for a brief moment, wishing this was all a dream. He could already sense trouble following his mother right to his door.

"I've heard so much about her since I've been here that I was excited to finally meet her."

Of course, he'd heard about her. No secret was safe around Orvyn. Blaze had caught the man more than once conversing with the villagers when he was supposed to be working. He was also sure the man had spoken to each man and woman in his service about his mother by now. This wasn't going well at all.

"Did you tell anyone at all that Lady Minerva returned to stay at Skull Manor?"

"Stay? She's going to be living here then? Oh, I didn't know that, my lord. I thought she was just here for a visit. How nice this must be for you."

"Mmph," Blaze grunted. Egads, he was feeding the man information and making things worse without even realizing what he was doing. All he'd meant to do was to find out what Orvyn knew. Well, now he knew even more thanks to him.

"Orvyn, this is her home too, after all. She only left for a while but she's back now."

"Ah, I heard she left because she was blamed for the feud? How long has she been gone? After all, I've been here for over a year now and have never seen her so it must have been for quite some time, I'm guessing."

"Five years," he said, just wanting to shut the man up.

"Five years." Orvyn whistled. "That is quite a long time not to have seen your own mother."

"Yes."

"You know, I've heard some weird things about her. Some of the villagers and servants even say your mother is a witch." He forced a laugh. "I'm sure they just mean she has been hard on them at one time or another, my lord."

"Yes. I'm sure."

"Then you won't be wanting your horse saddled? Mayhap you and your mother will be going for a ride together now that she's home?"

"Nay. And please don't say a word about my mother being here to anyone," Blaze reminded him. He didn't need an uproar from the village or the rest of his household. His mother wasn't very popular anymore since the feud started.

"Of course I won't, my lord. But may I ask, why not?" Orvyn's interest seemed suddenly peaked. Blaze's mind ran rampant with all kinds of thoughts of what this man was going to run around telling people now.

"She just . . . likes her privacy, that's all. I'm sure you understand."

"Well, not really, since she is the lady of the castle. I'd think she'd want to make more of a presence here."

"Still, will you please just keep her arrival to yourself?"

"If that's what you wish, my lord." The man looked severely put out, but bowed anyway. "Will there be anything else?"

"Aye. Saddle my horse after all. I changed my mind. I think I will go for a ride.

After he was finally able to get away from the manor, Blaze rode his horse through the forest, letting the wind whip through his hair. The day had become much colder since before the storm earlier. Winter would be approaching soon, and it looked as if another storm was brewing and about to begin.

The wind bit at his face but he didn't care. He needed to clear his head. Having his mother back in his life was jarring. He wasn't sure just how to handle this. She'd made such a mess of things before she left, and he'd only just started to feel as if he had hope again. Now, he felt like he was the one who wanted to leave, just so he didn't have to deal with the rumors that the witch was back. He knew what would follow. Everyone would be calling him a warlock again soon.

Blaze found himself back at the cemetery without realizing where he was headed. The little graveyard was just outside St. Basil's church. It wasn't a very large church, but still a good size for the surroundings. It was situated between his home and Lillith's. It was a place that he and she used to ride to years ago when they were children, pretending they were going there to be wed.

He spotted Huntley riding away from the graveyard and Lillith was on her horse right behind him. They were headed in the direction of Alderwood Castle. Lillith's home. This made him curious as to why Lillith had returned to her father's burial place so soon. Blaze followed them but kept just out of sight. He'd been thinking about Lillith and then she suddenly appeared. God's eyes, he wondered if he'd done this. After all, his mother had just been telling him that he created his own luck, plus other such things.

Blaze rode in silence, watching Lillith's elegance atop her horse. She sat sidesaddle as was proper of a lady. Her blue gown was covered by a long dark blue cloak that hung over the sides of her horse. With her back straight and her composure elite, she rode with her head held high. She looked straight forward, never even seeing him following in the shadows. Her loose, black hair fell in a soft cascade of waves over her shoulders making him wonder if it still smelled like lilies of the valley or if it was still as soft as silk. He smiled to himself remembering how he used to tease her, telling her she was his little lily flower. She'd never liked the name Lillith, but when he'd called her Lilly it had seemed to please her.

They stopped near the creek. Huntley took the horses to the

water to drink while Lillith sat down on a rock and fixed her shoe. Blaze rode up quietly behind her, just meaning to watch from the brush, but she heard him.

"Who goes there?" she blurted out, jumping up with her dagger in hand. Her eyes squinted and she looked directly in his direction. If he wasn't mistaken, she sounded scared. It was dusk now and at first she didn't recognize him as he rode forward to make his presence known. But when his raven swooped down from the sky and landed on the pommel of his saddle, she had no doubt as to his identity.

"Ebony?" she said, looking at the raven, calling it by name. Lillith loved animals, and always seemed to have a connection with his pet. Then she stepped backwards and gasped. "Blaze," she said in a breathy whisper, her big blue eyes opening wide in surprise. Seeing her this close made him realize just how much she'd grown into a woman in the past five years, and just how much he'd missed her. Her body had all the right curves now, although she still held that sparkle of innocence about her. Just hearing her voice again after all this time was music to his ears. It sent a surge of excitement flowing through him.

"Hello, Lilly," he answered with a nod, sliding off his horse and slowly walking over to meet her.

"What are you doing here? Are you following me?" She took another step backward as if he scared her, stumbling on the rock she'd sat on earlier. Blaze shot forward and grabbed on to her arm, pulling her closer to him to keep her from falling.

For one magical moment he felt like it was five years earlier and that there had never been any trouble between their families at all. He stared deeply into her eyes, able to read all her emotions just like always. As she stared back at him, he felt her caution and realized she still grasped her dagger behind her back. She didn't trust him. He also read the feeling of despair mixed with a curious nature to be in his arms again.

For a second she almost seemed happy. Then, the scared look

returned and her eyes became dark and angry. Lillith lifted her chin high in the air, in an unspoken challenge.

"What do you want?" she demanded to know. Now, her back stiffened and her entire appearance changed. The sparkling innocence and kindness he'd witnessed was gone. In its place was a cold stare from squinted eyes that sent a shiver to replace the warmth of excitement he'd felt a moment ago just from being near her.

"It's been so long since I've seen you, Lilly. You are even more beautiful than when we last parted."

One eyebrow raised as she perused him from head to foot. He'd almost expected her to return the compliment, but she didn't. Instead, she spoke to him through clenched teeth.

"I said, what do you want?"

"Why are you out here alone at dusk and without an escort?" His eyes scanned the area, but Huntley was still down at the creek. If he were a bandit, he could have easily robbed her or even abducted her by now.

"I'm not alone. I have Huntley with me."

"Really," he said with a chuckle.

Her eyes flashed toward the creek and then back to him. She pulled out of his embrace, making distance between them and yanked the dagger out from behind her back pointing the blade toward him. "I can protect myself," she told him as the dagger in her hand shook.

"You have an undertaker with you who left you unguarded, but no guards from the castle?" He raised a brow. "I find that curious, sweetheart."

She waved her dagger closer to him as she answered. "Why would I need guards?"

"For protection, Lilly Bee."

"Don't call me that!" Her eyes opened wide again. "My name is Lillith, and you know it."

"I also know you don't like being called Lillith, but you adore it when I call you my little Lilly."

"Stop it. It's over between us," she said, sounding like she meant it.

He could have kicked himself for using his pet name for her now. Or at least the Bee part after the Lilly. The girl's middle name was Beatrice, so he'd made up an endearment for her that she used to love. Now, it only seemed to infuriate her.

"Why did you come back to the graveyard?" he asked.

"Why did you?" came her tart reply. "Did you have something to do with my father's death?" she asked him bluntly.

This surprised Blaze and his heart dropped. So, it seemed that Milo knew he'd been the one bending over her father's dead body after all. Damn. He had been hoping that the boy didn't know.

"Is that what you really think?" he asked her. "That I could kill someone like your father?" He moved closer and she moved farther away.

"You're a warlock," she spat. "And your mother is a witch." She crinkled her nose as if just saying this aloud repulsed her.

"I see you've inherited your father's attitudes and opinions."

"Are you denying it?"

He didn't know what to say. He couldn't agree to this, because it would only mean trouble for his family if he did. Yet, he didn't want to lie to her either. He'd kept the secret for much too long, and it had never felt right to begin with. Part of him regretted not telling her years ago when she was so much more accepting of him.

"Whether you believe it or not, I had nothing to do with the death of your father," he said, rather than to address the issue of witches.

"Really."

"I have no qualms with your family. I never have," he told her. "It was our fathers who were feuding. It never should have involved us."

"That's a lie. Your mother cursed Robert and now he's dead." The wench sounded as if she really believed this nonsense. My, had she changed. At one time Lillith had a mind of her own and would never think ill thoughts about him or his family. Now he couldn't get her to think or say a kind thing about him.

"Nay. That's not true. My mother didn't curse anyone. Plus, I never wanted trouble between us, I swear. I care about you, Lilly. In case you've forgotten, that man in the wooden box that was buried today was not only your father, but was almost my father by marriage."

"Nay, he wasn't. Don't say that. I would never marry a warlock." Why was she being so stubborn and acting this way? He really missed the old Lilly.

"Our fathers had a verbal agreement that one day we'd be betrothed," he reminded her.

"It wasn't in writing and meant nothing," she spat.

"If it wasn't for the feud, we would have married one day, and you know it."

"Never. That was nothing but a childhood infatuation." Her face remained stone-like but at least she lowered the dagger a little.

"Was it really only infatuation, or something much more?" he asked her. "Were all those plans we had of spending our life together nothing but a fantasy or was it what we both really wanted?"

"Stop it," she said in a whisper, her eyes partially closing. She seemed to be holding her breath. She couldn't look at him when he asked this, so he knew she didn't mean all those nasty things after all. He watched a blush rise to her cheeks, and knew for certain she was lying. She still had feelings for him, just like he did for her.

"We cared for each other, sweetheart, and you know it. Don't try to deny it because I don't believe that at all."

The wind blew a stray strand of her ebony hair across her face. Without thinking what he was doing, he stepped forward, reaching out and gently brushing it back behind her ear. Her arm went limp and she lowered the blade to her side. When his fingers grazed against her soft skin, it became spellbinding and he couldn't look away. One more gentle stroke of her cheek and

Lillith's eyes closed completely and her head fell back. This only reminded Blaze of the first, and only time he'd kissed Lillith. It was something he'd never forget. She was so sweet, and he was so unsure of himself around her. Part of him longed to go right back to those when life was so much easier.

The scent of lilies of the valley drifted from her body. It was the perfume he'd had an herbalist make up for her years ago from the oil of the flowers because of her name. He'd given it to her as a special gift on her fifteenth birthday, just before all the trouble between them started. He found it interesting that she still wore the scent. Especially since their families had been feuding for such a long time.

Blaze was trapped in his memories of the past and couldn't stop himself from cupping her cheek in his palm. He liked the way it felt to touch her again. It felt right and natural. He hadn't had eyes for anyone but her since this whole stupid feud began.

With her eyes still closed, she turned her head and slowly nuzzled his hand with her nose. He swore he heard her moan slightly. Boldly, Blaze took a step even closer.

When he did, her eyes drifted open, and he found himself looking directly at her, close enough to kiss her. His gaze fell to her pink lips with that full bottom lip and cute little natural pout that always drove him mad.

That's when he noticed her looking at his mouth too. Throwing caution to the wind, he leaned in and gently brushed his lips across hers in a quick kiss. He wasn't all that sure she wouldn't stab him with her dagger, so he was cautious – the same way he was the first time he'd kissed her so many years ago. He didn't want to frighten her, but he wanted her to know she was safe with him by her side. Blaze wanted to show her that nothing between them had changed after all. Or at least, not on his end, it hadn't.

His fond memories of the past as well as his hope was knocked right out of his head when he felt her palm slapping across his cheek hard. It stung more than the autumn wind against his face.

The action startled his raven. The bird began to hiss from atop the horse, flapping its large wings wildly.

"How dare you!" she retorted.

That took him aback. He wasn't expecting her to react this way and wasn't exactly sure what to do or say now.

"I'm sorry," he blurted out, quickly stepping away from her, making distance between them. He'd never have kissed her if he didn't think she'd like it. He looked up to see Huntley running back from the creek now, holding the reins of the horses that trailed behind him.

"Lady Lillith, is there a problem?" called out Huntley, stretching his neck, trying to see better. "I thought I heard something." Blaze purposely kept his face turned away from the undertaker, not wanting Huntley to know he was there.

"It's the warlock," gasped Huntley, recognizing Blaze immediately, and stopping dead in his tracks. Damn, too late. "I'll protect you, Lady Lillith." Huntley nervously fumbled for his dagger, but it got tangled in his cloak. Blaze took this as his cue to leave. Huntley couldn't protect a mouse let alone a damsel in distress. Still, Blaze gave him credit for trying. Blaze didn't want trouble, and decided to just leave.

"Huntley, for God's sake, put away your blade," he said over his shoulder, heading back to his horse. "I would never hurt Lady Lillith, and you know it." He took one last look at the beautiful woman from his past, and then pulled himself up into his saddle. His raven squawked and took off into the sky. "I'm sorry, Lilly," he said in a low voice. "I thought it was what you wanted."

"What does that mean?" asked Huntley, finally getting a grip on his blade and holding his dagger out in front of him as he moved closer to Lillith.

Blaze didn't think Lillith was going to answer. But as he turned to ride away, he heard her mumble her answer. "At one time, it was what I wanted, but not anymore."

Blaze rode away, his heart breaking to hear her say this. His life of living hell for the last five years wasn't over after all. Actually, now it seemed as if it was never going to end.

Lillith's hand went to her cheek as she watched Blaze ride away. As she ran her fingers over her face, she could still feel the essence of his touch on her skin. She could also still taste the lingering flavor of his soft but strong lips that he'd gently brushed up against hers.

Blaze had caught her off guard when he'd touched her. It was the last thing she ever expected to happen. His gentle caress brought back feelings she thought she'd buried long ago. When their lips met, it made her body come back to life. She'd felt dead, ignoring her emotions ever since the feud started. But now, something deep inside her screamed to be with Blaze, while another part of her warned her to stay far, far away.

"My lady, did he hurt you?" asked Huntley, waving his dagger in the air as Blaze rode away. "I'll stab him if he comes back, I swear I will."

"Nay, I'm fine," said Lillith, running her tongue over her lips to savor his taste. Her mouth held the faint flavor of whisky. The strong scent of Blaze's leather clothes still lingered in the air around her. It made her want him to turn around and come back. "Let's go," she said, turning to mount her horse, angry at herself for even allowing him to kiss her. Why did she turn to clay in this warlock's hands? How did it seem she still had feelings for him when she'd worked so hard to convince herself that she no longer cared?

"My lady, you must remember that Lord Blaze might have had something to do with your father's death since he and his bloody blade were both seen at the site. Besides, he is your mortal enemy now, and also a warlock." Huntley reminded her.

"I know, Huntley," she answered, watching Blaze's long cloak billowing out behind him as he rode away fast and disappeared from sight. "I guess for a moment I just thought I was with someone else."

Four

"SISTER, where have you been so long?" asked Serena, meeting Lillith as she rode into the courtyard. Huntley had left her at the gate and gone back to his village. "I was getting worried."

"Did you tell anyone where I went?"

"Nay," said Serena. "If I had, it would only have caused trouble with Uncle Arthur."

"Lillith? Were you out alone this late?" asked her mother, walking across the courtyard to join them with Arthur at her side. Her handmaid, Posy followed at her heels.

"Yes. Where have you been? Your mother was worried sick about you." Arthur didn't really seem upset that she'd been missing, but acted as if he were trying to sound concerned for her mother's sake or just to put on a show.

"I wasn't alone," she told them. "And if you must know, I went to the graveyard to pay Huntley the money he was owed for his services." Lillith had to tell them something so figured it might as well be the truth.

"You did what?" Arthur's bushy brows furrowed. "I said the undertaker would wait until morning for his pay, yet you went behind my back and did it anyway?" Now, Arthur seemed angry.

"Well, Serena and I didn't agree with you," Lillith answered, realizing by Serena's expression that she hadn't appreciated being included in this confrontation at all.

"I am your father now, and you'll ask me for permission to leave the castle from now on," growled Arthur.

"You will never be our father, even when you do marry our mother," Lillith answered for them both. "Besides, we've never had to ask permission before to go riding. We're not children anymore."

"Well, things are different now that I am lord," snapped Arthur. "You will go nowhere unescorted and will report to me before and after you go anywhere outside the castle's walls."

"Arthur, don't you think you're being a little harsh?" asked Beatrice softly. "After all, the girls are adults now and shouldn't be treated like children."

"That's right." Serena finally spoke. "Lillith will even be married soon."

"You're of marrying age too, Lady Serena," Arthur pointed out. "As a matter of fact, I think it's time you're both betrothed. I'll see to it right away."

"What?" Serena's eyes darted over to Lillith. She pleaded silently for help.

"Serena doesn't know any men that she can marry," said Lillith, not knowing how to help her.

"Arthur, it's really too close to Henri's death to be thinking about all this right now," added her mother.

"My lady, would you like me to accompany your daughters into the keep and help them prepare for bed?" asked Posy.

The handmaid was about the age of Beatrice. She had always tended to the needs of Serena and Lillith as well as their mother, although the girls didn't need it.

"Yes, thank you, Posy," said Beatrice, sniffling and dabbing her nose with a cloth. It would take a long time for any of them to come to terms with the death of Lillith's father.

"Wait," said Lillith, not wanting to leave before she settled things with her uncle. "Uncle Arthur, I heard that Milo saw a man leaning over Father's body. Is this true?"

"What? I didn't know this," said her mother, becoming very upset. "Arthur, why didn't you tell me?"

"It means nothing, and there was no sense mentioning it," remarked Arthur.

"There might have been foul play involved." Beatrice wrung her hands together in worry.

"Nonsense. My brother had a bad heart, not to mention he'd been drinking heavily," said Arthur. "The pageboy found him dead on the ground, having fallen off his horse and onto his own hunting knife. His death was naught but a freak accident."

"But what about the man Milo saw?" asked Serena. "Who was he and why was he there?"

"I'm sure the boy just imagined the whole thing," Arthur answered, trying to dismiss the matter. "He was so scared he was shaking like a leaf when he returned to the castle to tell me about it."

"Arthur, mayhap you should look into this better," suggested Lillith's mother.

"It wasn't foul play," insisted Arthur. "I saw it for myself. Henri's own bloody blade was next to him, after he must have pulled it out of his gut. He also seemed to have hit his head on a rock when he fell drunk from his horse. My brother never was smart when it came to his health. He always loved to go riding alone in the dark when he was soused. I'll never understand it."

"Mayhap the warlock killed him," said Posy, not afraid to speak freely.

"Warlock?" Beatrice looked up in confusion.

"That's who Milo said he saw," answered the woman.

"Are you saying Lord Payne had something to do with my husband's death?"

"Nay, of course not," protested Arthur. "If you ask me, the boy is just trying to start trouble. I was there and saw no one else."

"I'm scared," cried Serena, taking a hold of her mother's arm.

Lillith realized now that she never should have said a thing. This was how rumors started and feuds began. She was no better than any of the wagging tongues around the castle. Lillith regretted not just keeping this information to herself. Now everyone was going to do nothing but worry about something that probably meant nothing at all, just like Arthur said.

"I'd like to hear more, but from Milo." Beatrice called Milo over.

Milo was a thirteen-year-old page who had always been a good friend of the family. There had never been any reason to doubt his word.

"My lord. My lady," said Milo with a bow.

"Milo, did you see Lord Payne near my husband on the road the day he died?" asked Beatrice.

"I – I'm not exactly sure," said the boy, shifting from foot to foot. "I thought I saw someone in a cloak leaning over his body and then they were gone."

"I'm sure he just imagined the whole thing," said Arthur.

"I saw something else too," said Milo.

"That'll be all," said Arthur in a dismissing manner.

"Nay, wait." Beatrice stopped him. "I'd like to hear everything. After all, this is my husband we're talking about."

"I saw a dagger lying near Lord Bonnel," continued Milo. "I mean, if that's who I saw."

"If you saw a dagger, why didn't you pick it up?" asked Arthur.

"I was going to, but the look of it frightened me."

"How in heaven's name could a dagger scare you?" asked Arthur with a roll of his eyes. "God's eyes, you're too fragile to even be a simple page."

"Arthur, please," begged Beatrice. "Milo is a good friend of the family. If he said he saw something, I have no reason not to believe him."

"I didn't want to touch the dagger because it was bloody and I didn't want to be cursed," Milo finally admitted, looking as white as a ghost.

"What?" asked Beatrice.

"It was the warlock's dagger, I'm sure of it." Milo's eyes grew wide. "I've seen him carrying it in the past."

"Now, that's nonsense," said Arthur. "All daggers basically look alike. How would you know who it belonged to?"

"Nay, this one is different," Milo told them. "This one had moons and stars on the hilt as well as a skull right on the end of it. It is terrifying, I tell you."

Lillith had been at Skull Manor when Blaze's mother gave him the blade many years ago, so she knew Milo was telling the truth.

"So, the Paynes are once again responsible for the death of a member of our family," said Beatrice, crying and dabbing her eyes once again.

"I don't think Blaze would kill father, or anyone for that matter." Lillith surprised herself by saying this aloud.

"Lillith, you're only saying that because you're still in love with him," said Serena.

"Nay, I'm not. But Blaze is not a bad person. At least, I don't think," she added softly, wondering why she'd felt so frightened around him earlier today. Perhaps it was just all the talk she'd heard for the last five years about Blaze's family being witches. Her father had a vengeance for that, and wanted Blaze's family to burn at the stake. Lillith would never agree to that, no matter if they were witches or not.

"Henri wouldn't have been feuding with the Paynes if they were to be trusted," said Beatrice.

"Mayhap not," Lillith answered softly, not sure what to think anymore.

"Well, now that I'm Lord of Alderwood, there will be no more feuding," stated Arthur. "This has gone on much too long. Didn't you say Lord Payne just died as well?"

"He did," said Serena.

"Then, I think it's time the feud dies with them," said Arthur.

"Arthur, how do you expect to make that happen?" asked Beatrice.

"I know exactly how to do it. All we need is to make an alliance."

"An alliance?" asked Serena. "That sounds like you mean a betrothal."

"I do."

"But Uncle, you said Lillith is betrothed to the baron." Serena shook her head in confusion.

"Yes, that's right, Arthur. We can't break the betrothal," said Beatrice. "Henri wouldn't want us to. It could cause dire issues for us if we go back on our word. We need to honor the agreement or risk starting a feud with the baron."

"We won't break it," said Arthur. "Lillith isn't your only daughter of marrying age, Beatrice. Serena is unwed too. She'll marry Lord Blaze Payne instead."

"What?" asked Lillith, feeling somewhat slighted. After all, she was the one who used to be in love with Blaze, not Serena.

"Me? Nay," cried Serena. "I don't want to marry a warlock." She seemed mortified by the idea. "Please, Uncle, don't do this to me."

"Blaze would never agree to it," said Lillith quickly, knowing Blaze's feelings for her.

"I'll take care of that," said Arthur with a grin. "I'll send a messenger with a missive to his manor tonight and by tomorrow Serena will be betrothed just like you, Lillith."

"Oh," said Lillith, her heart sinking. This wasn't at all what she wanted. Blaze meant nothing to Serena and Lillith was sure he didn't want to marry her either. The alliance was not going to work. Even if the idea of ending the feud did intrigue her, they still weren't even sure they could trust Blaze and his family right now. Her father didn't think so, and Lillith had inherited his feelings during the past five years. After all, if Blaze was a warlock and never told her, who knew what else he was hiding?

After thinking about some of the things she saw at Skull Manor when she was growing up as best friends with Blaze, she had no doubt in her mind that they truly were witches.

Her uncle always acted impulsively, and this time it was going to end badly, she was sure.

"I don't think this is the best idea right now, Uncle Arthur," she told him, not caring that women weren't supposed to speak their minds.

"Why not? It'll solve all our problems, not to mention you two girls will finally be married," said Arthur.

Lillith was sure he really meant it would solve all his problems and that he'd finally be rid of them.

"I've been telling Henri for years that you two were getting too old and should have been married years ago. No man is going to want you much longer." Arthur blew air from his mouth and he shook his head as if he were disgusted. "If you were my daughters, you would have been married at twelve or thirteen – the proper age for a noble to marry. I have no idea why Henri waited so long."

"It's too soon after Father's death to even be discussing this," protested Lillith. "I think we should wait with any more betrothals."

"Well, I don't," snapped Arthur.

"Mother?" Lillith looked to her mother for support, but the woman was in no position to contest Arthur's decision. She was still distraught over losing her husband. And like she mentioned to Lillith, if she wanted to keep from losing her home, she had no choice but to become Arthur's bride.

"I'm sorry girls, but if Arthur thinks this is best, then I have to agree with him."

"Nay, Mother. Please," begged Serena, looking like she was about to swoon.

"What about all this talk of Blaze being a warlock? And Milo seeing Blaze's bloody dagger next to Father's body?" asked Lillith grasping for excuses to stop her sister's betrothal.

"I told you, that is nothing to worry about," snapped Arthur. "I'm sure there is a good reason for everything and we all need to stop speculating right now."

"Even if he's a warlock and his mother is a witch?" asked Serena.

"Bah!" Arthur waved his hand through the air. "They are not. I'm surprised you really believe that idle gossip."

"Father believed it," said Serena.

"Henri was always superstitious, but I'm not," said Arthur. "I've made my decision and it is final. Now, I'll not hear another word about it."

"Ladies Serena and Lillith, perhaps you would like to retire to your chamber now," said Posy, trying to direct them toward the keep.

"Yes," agreed their mother. "I'll be retiring as well. It has been a horrible day and I can only hope tomorrow will be better."

"Page, bring the scribe back to my solar to write a missive for me," Arthur told Milo. "And then I'll need you to deliver it to Lord Blaze Payne at Skull Manor."

"Me?" Milo's eyes opened wide. "Tonight?"

"You're a page aren't you?" growled Arthur.

"Yes, but I don't normally deliver messages. That's usually done by one of the guards or a messenger," said Milo.

"Well, tonight you're going to do it. Unless you're scared of Lord Blaze," he said with a chuckle. "If you can't toughen up, you'll never be more than a pageboy."

"I'm not scared if that's what you think. I'll do it," said Milo with false bravado. Lillith noticed him biting his bottom lip. Milo always did that when he was told to do something he didn't feel comfortable with. Still, he longed to be a squire someday and knew he had to be brave to earn that position.

"Uncle Arthur? Please don't do this," said Lillith.

"Lillith, you're not going to be devastated that I'm offering your sister to your lover, are you?" asked Arthur, surprising Lillith with his words.

"Blaze was never my lover. Just a good friend at one time," she said softly, not able to stop thinking about how she felt when he'd touched her and kissed her less than an hour ago. "He means nothing to me anymore," she lied, not wanting her uncle to know how much this idea was really upsetting her.

"Good," said Arthur. "Because as soon as I get Lord Payne's answer saying he accepts the proposal, I'm going to send you to Skull Manor with Serena."

"Me? Why?" she asked, feeling her heart race.

"It'll only be until the wedding takes place," said Arthur. "After all, your sister will be too frightened to meet up with the man alone, so she'll most likely need to hold your hand."

Lillith felt bile rising in her throat, threatening to choke her. She didn't want to go. She couldn't do it. The only thought that calmed her down was that she knew Blaze would never agree to marrying Serena.

Five

"MY LORD, this missive just arrived for you." Barnaby stopped him in the courtyard with a folded-up piece of parchment in his hand. It was dark outside since the moon was hiding behind clouds, and Blaze wouldn't be able to read it here.

"A messenger just delivered it? This late?" asked Blaze in confusion. Who in their right mind would send a messenger out at night? Especially so near All Hallows' Eve which was coming up in a few days' time.

"It surprised me too," said Barnaby.

"Is it from the Earl of Birmingham?" asked Blaze, feeling nervous and excited at the same time. He had been waiting for a reply from the earl since his father's funeral. Blaze's father had been the earl's head knight, so of course Earl Cyriac of Birmingham attended the services. It was only because of the earl's presence that the church even let his father be buried on consecrated ground. Blaze was thankful for the man's help. His father deserved a proper burial.

Blaze had approached the earl afterwards about being knighted and taking over his father's position. Or any position of knight, actually. Five long years had given Blaze the opportunity to finish his training on his own.

The earl had told him he'd think about it and let Blaze know his answer soon. Blaze hoped it wasn't just a brush-off. He also hoped this missive wasn't the earl turning him down.

"Nay, my lord, it's not from the earl," said his steward. "A messenger from Alderwood Castle delivered it."

"Alderwood?" This took Blaze's interest more than anything. "Let me see that," he said, taking the folded parchment from the man and walking over to a torch to break the wax seal and read it in the firelight. He had no idea why he'd be receiving a missive from there. Part of him hoped it was from Lillith. After seeing her and kissing her today, he'd been able to think of nothing else.

"What's that, Blaze? Is someone sending you a missive?" His mother moseyed out of the manor, not caring that she was in plain view of anyone.

"Mother," he said, blowing a puff of air from his mouth. "I thought I told you to stay inside."

"Lady Minerva, I didn't know you'd returned," said Barnaby in surprise, bowing to the woman.

"Yes, I'm here to stay. Even though my son would rather keep me hidden," scoffed Minerva.

"Thank you, Barnaby," said Blaze, dismissing the man. He decided there was no use now trying to keep his mother's presence a secret, or even trying to send her away. It was obvious she was going nowhere and Blaze didn't want to fight her on it. Some of his servants as well as his guards were already curiously looking in their direction. Hushed conversations started up and Blaze knew exactly what they were about. Orvyn walked out of the stable, hurrying over and half-bowing.

"My lord and lady," said Orvyn. "I'm so happy that Lady Minerva's presence is no longer a secret."

"Believe me, it's not by my doing," grunted Blaze, quickly scanning the contents of the parchment.

"What does the missive say?" asked Minerva. "And who is it from?"

"It's from Alderwood Castle," said Orvyn before Blaze could

even answer. He didn't bother asking Orvyn how he knew. The stables were near the front gate. Nothing escaped Orvyn's attention.

Blaze read the rest of the missive and his lips pursed up into a smile.

"Is it good news or bad?" asked Minerva.

"I'd say it's good news since Lord Blaze is smiling." Once again, Orvyn answered.

Blaze sighed and folded the missive back up. "Orvyn, since you're only going to start gossip about this missive if I don't tell you its contents, I'm just going to reveal to you what it's all about."

"Oh, you don't need to do that. It's really none of my business," said Orvyn, his eyes roaming back to the missive. "Unless you want to, of course."

"Well, I want him to tell us," said Minerva sternly. "Son, what do the Bonnels want with us? Whatever it is, I'm sure it's trouble."

"Nay, actually it's not," he enjoyed saying to his mother. "They want to form an alliance with us to end the feud."

"An alliance? End the feud?" asked Orvyn, nodding in surprise. "That's good. Right?"

"Exactly what kind of alliance?" asked Minerva suspiciously, looking from the corners of her eyes.

"Lord Arthur Bonnel – the new lord of the castle, has offered me the hand of his niece in marriage," answered Blaze, feeling as if things were finally starting to look up after all.

"Marriage? Really? That's exceptional, my lord," said Orvyn giving his approval, even though Blaze couldn't care less what the man thought.

"His niece?" asked Minerva. "Which one? He has two, you know."

Blaze opened and read over the missive once again. "He doesn't actually say. It only says Lady Bonnel, but I'm sure he means Lady Lillith. After all, she is the eldest and is still not married. Plus, we once planned on marrying each other. Our fathers made a verbal promise between them."

"I remember," mumbled Beatrice.

"Well, I guess it's finally going to happen after all. It seems my luck is changing." He surprised his mother by leaning over and kissing her on the cheek. He supposed she wasn't really a bad luck charm after all.

"How are you going to answer, my lord? Will you accept the offer?" asked Orvyn being so out of line even asking these questions. Still, Blaze was so happy now that he didn't even reprimand the man.

"Will you? Will you say yes?" asked Minerva.

Blaze thought about it for a minute. This all seemed so surreal. After so many years of feuding with the Bonnels, and after their accusations of Blaze's family being witches and cursing their son who died, Blaze didn't think they'd ever come to terms again.

"I don't know," said Blaze. "I find this all so hard to believe. Plus, it's so sudden after Henri's death that it's almost a little odd. It doesn't seem like something the Bonnels would even consider. Especially after the rumors that they've heard about our family. Henri was very adamant that his daughters would never go near me again."

"This missive didn't come from Henri," Minerva reminded him, as if she really needed to.

"I've heard Henri's brother Arthur is quite different from Henri. He's known to be impulsive," said Orvyn.

"Aye, I guess so. After all, he sent a messenger so soon after the death of his brother, and in the middle of the night." Blaze shook his head, not sure what to think. Part of him warned him to use caution, but another part was too excited to do anything but to accept the proposal and make Lillith his wife.

"Mayhap the feud will finally be over," said Orvyn. "I mean, Lord Arthur didn't have ill feelings toward you and your family, did he?"

"I suppose not," said Blaze in thought, staring down at the

missive that could change his life. "I actually don't really know the man at all."

"Do you think you can trust the Bonnels?" asked Minerva. "Mayhap this is some sort of trap or just a ploy to hurt us."

"Nay. I don't think so," said Blaze shaking his head and folding the missive back up. It did make sense, he decided. Henri was gone and so was Blaze's father. Mayhap the feud had died along with them. After all, it had been Blaze's father who fought with Henri, not Blaze. And even though Lillith slapped him today, he supposed he deserved it for his improper behavior of kissing her in public. She didn't mean anything by it, he was sure. He'd seen it in her eyes that she truly did enjoy his kiss. Perhaps it was Lillith who convinced her uncle to make this alliance after all. "I believe this is a legitimate attempt to make things right between our families."

"Then you'll be accepting the offer of marriage?" asked Minerva.

"Mother, I have waited a long time to make amends with the Bonnels and for things to be the way they used to be. Yes, I believe I will accept the offer. It is what's best for both the Bonnels as well as the Paynes. Orvyn, find my scribe and send him to my solar. I will write my reply and send it back to Lord Arthur right away. Tonight," he added with a nod, feeling happy and as impulsive right now as Lord Arthur Bonnel.

"Aye, my lord," said Orvyn, bowing quickly and running off to find the scribe.

"Blaze, are you sure this is a good idea?" asked his mother in concern.

"Yes, it is." He headed toward the keep and she followed.

"Well, I'm not sure. I still don't trust them. Mayhap you should take a day or two to ponder it over."

"Mother, you're not going to change my mind. And don't bother consulting your cards, because I won't listen to any kind of warning you might read into the situation."

"But my cards are never wrong. I think it would be wise to consult them."

He stopped in his tracks, causing his mother to almost crash into him since she'd been so close. "Nay! Now, I won't hear another word about it. I'm going to marry Lillith Bonnel, and you won't talk me out of it. As soon as my missive reaches Arthur, the deal will be finalized. This is my time to start over. I will start fresh with a new life that includes my precious Lilly as my wife. That is what was always meant to be."

"You are too trusting, Blaze," Minerva scolded. "You're too infatuated with the girl to think about this objectively. I don't want to see you hurt. I have a bad feeling about this and beg you not to accept the offer."

"Just keep your feelings to yourself, Mother. This alliance is going to open doors for me that have been slammed in my face and closed for a long time now. Once Earl Birmingham hears that the Bonnel family is aligned with us, he'll accept me as his knight eagerly, with no doubt in his mind. I'll follow in my father's footsteps after all."

"Send your missive then, and marry the girl if that is what you think you should do. I still think you should reject the proposal. Then again, when have you ever listened to me before?"

"It has never proved beneficial for me to listen to you in the past, and I sure as hell am not going to start now." Blaze walked away, eager to get away from his mother and to set the plans in motion for marrying his sweet little Lilly.

* * *

"I can't marry Lord Blaze Payne, Uncle. Please, don't make me do it," pleaded Serena, still trying to convince her uncle to change his mind the next morning.

Lillith sat next to her sister at the dais as they shared a meal to break the fast.

"Don't worry, Serena," said Lillith, taking a sip of mead. "I know Blaze well enough to realize he'll never accept this deal."

"Don't be so sure." Arthur didn't seem at all worried. He sat back with a smug look on his face and his hands on his belly, just having finished his meal. Her uncle looked much too content in their castle sitting in her father's chair. Lillith didn't like this.

"What does that mean?" asked Lillith suspiciously, getting the feeling there was something that her uncle was not telling her.

"Arthur, please. Tell her," begged her mother.

"Tell me what?" asked Lillith, putting down her cup. "What is it, Uncle?"

"I received an answer back from Lord Blaze late last night."

"You did?" asked Lillith, thinking it odd that Blaze should answer so quickly and not wait until morning. It wasn't like him to be so unpredictable.

"He accepted the proposal," announced Arthur, leaving Lillith lost for words. Her jaw dropped and she felt sick to her stomach. "The final papers are going to be sent this morning to be signed, and the alliance will be set in motion."

"Nay!" cried Serena. "This can't be happening. My life is over."

"Hush, Serena," scolded Lillith, looking back over to her uncle. "Can I see the proposal Blaze signed?" she asked, not willing to believe it was true until she saw Blaze's signature on that parchment.

"Don't you believe me, dear?" asked Arthur.

"I just want to see it, that's all," she answered.

"Arthur, please. Have the steward show it to her. He's right here."

"Sir Gunderic, bring that parchment over to my niece so she can see that I'm not the liar she thinks I am," he growled.

"Aye, my lord." Sir Gunderic walked to the front of the dais and handed Lillith a rolled-up piece of parchment with two hands as was proper.

With one shaking hand Lillith took it from him and slowly

unrolled it to read the proposal. Her eyes moved back and forth as she read the writing on the page.

"Uncle, you only mention the betrothed as Lady Bonnel. You didn't tell him which one of us he is marrying." To her dismay, there at the bottom of the paper was Blaze's signature.

"I guess it didn't matter to him. Now give me that before something happens to it." Arthur reached over and snatched it out of her hand.

Now it all made sense to Lillith. Blaze had thought he was signing an agreement to marry her, she was sure of it. If he had known he was being tricked into marrying Serena, he never would have been so fast to sign it.

"Now that the meal is finished, you two will pack your bags and go. Milo will take you over to Skull Manor," Arthur told her.

"Oh, Lillith, I'm so glad you're coming with me," said Serena, grabbing on to her arm. "I am so scared that Lord Blaze is going to curse me or even kill me."

"Don't be foolish. Blaze would never hurt a lady," she told her sister.

"Well, keep your dagger handy just in case the warlock comes for either of you in your sleep." Arthur laughed at his ill jest, but no one else thought it was funny.

"Arthur, how can you be so cold-hearted?" asked Beatrice.

"I'm only teasing your daughters, and mean nothing by it," said Arthur, reaching out and giving Beatrice's hand a squeeze.

"Still, I think they truly might be in danger," said Beatrice. "My husband always said not to trust the Bonnels. He swore they were witches."

"And what do you want me to do about this silly fear of yours?" asked Arthur.

"Mayhap you should send someone else along with the girls."

"You're right," said Arthur. He looked up and motioned across the room to the handmaid, Posy. The woman hurried over.

"Yes, my lord," said Posy with a smile. "You summoned me?"

"Aye," he answered. "Posy, you will accompany my nieces to

Skull Manor and stay with them until the wedding. Come back and get me if you discover the Paynes are dangerous witches."

"Me?" Posy's eyes opened wide. "Pardon me for saying that I don't fancy the idea, my lord. I don't want to be anywhere near Skull Manor."

"Lillith assures me that Lord Blaze and his family are harmless, so there is nothing to worry about now, is there?" Arthur chuckled again, causing Lillith to want to slap the smile right off his face. Her uncle cared naught about the safety of his newly acquired family. He was just in a hurry to get rid of them so he wouldn't have opposition to his decisions now that he was Lord of Alderwood. Lillith felt sorry for her mother who had no way of escaping the despicable man.

"Get moving, ladies. I've already sent word to Lord Payne that you'll be there first thing this morning," commanded Arthur getting up from his chair and stretching.

Lillith looked over to her mother who sadly shook her head. Her mother knew how much Blaze once meant to her. Lillith had often talked with her mother about what it would be like to one day be married to him. Now, none of that even mattered. Lillith was promised to the baron, not Blaze.

The thought of marrying someone besides Blaze made Lillith feel even worse now. She didn't want to be the one to tell him she was getting married. She also didn't want to be present when Blaze found out he'd been tricked by Arthur and that he'd willingly signed a betrothal to marry her sister, Serena.

Six

"NOW, listen, I don't want any trouble from you today when Lillith arrives," Blaze warned his mother. He sat down on the edge of his bed to don his boots while his mother, once again, spread out those blasted cards on his table.

"Oh!" she gasped, looking down at a card with wide eyes.

"I don't want to hear it." Blaze stood up with his hand in the air. He continued to strap on his weapon belt.

"Blaze, you need to hear this. It has to do with the betrothal."

"Nay. I told you, no more. Now put the cards away before I burn them."

"It's a warning. You need to know that –"

"Enough!" Blaze walked over, using his arm to swish all the cards to the floor. "Don't think I am jesting, because I'm not. Your silly ways and beliefs caused a feud years ago, but I am finally about to end it. Don't get in the way."

His mother scoffed, put down the deck and kneeled down to get the cards off the floor.

There came a knock on the door and then a muffled voice from the other side. "My lord," said his guard and good friend, Emery. "The Bonnel party has arrived and is waiting in the court-yard for you to greet them."

"I'll be right there," Blaze called back, hunkering down, hurriedly helping his mother retrieve the cards. When he handed them back to her, he noticed the Lovers card on the top. That made him smile. He wanted to be lovers with Lillith. He was so happy that they were finally betrothed. Blaze's life was about to change, and he was sure it would be for the better. "Hide these cards. I don't want the Bonnels to see them. Do you understand?"

"I think you ought to listen to what I have to say."

"Not now, Mother." Blaze hurried over and opened the door. "Emery, it's finally happening. I'm going to marry Lady Lillith," he said, excited about the idea.

"It's about time," said Emery with a chuckle. "Let's just hope after all this trouble, she'll be just as excited to marry you."

"She will," he told her. "I'm sure of it. Now, go and find my steward and send him out to the courtyard. He'll need to direct our guests to their rooms."

"Aye," said Emery, hurrying off to carry out his orders.

Blaze left the room, walking quickly out to the courtyard to meet his betrothed. He felt nervous in a way. After all, he hadn't talked to Lillith at all for the last five years. That is, before yesterday when he kissed her. And then she slapped him, he subtly reminded himself. Still, it didn't matter. All that mattered now was that they were betrothed, and she was here to stay.

This betrothal would change everything in his life. His old life would thankfully fade away and things would never be the same again.

"My lord, those people are the Bonnels, aren't they? The ones with whom you're in the middle of a feud?" Orvyn ran over, walking with him across the courtyard.

"Yes and no."

"What do you mean?"

"I mean, yes, they are the Bonnels. However, since I've accepted the betrothal proposal and will be marrying Lady Bonnel, I am making a well-needed alliance. The feud has finally come to an end."

"Well, that's great, my lord," said Orvyn. "Which one of the ladies are you marrying?"

"The beautiful one, of course." Blaze smiled, his eyes focused on no one but Lillith. He hurried over to the wagon, and stretched out his arm. "Allow me to help you, my lady," he said to Lillith, but her sister, Serena took his arm instead.

"Thank you, my lord. That is kind of you." Serena acted as if she thought he'd been talking to her.

Once she was out of the wagon, he repeated the action for Lillith. "So good to see you again, Lillith," he said with a smile, staring into her eyes. The odd part was, she wasn't smiling back at him the way he thought she would be. Instead, she looked upset. "Is something the matter?"

"We need to talk, Blaze."

"We'll have plenty of time for talking after we're married. I'm going to request that we don't wait the full three weeks as expected and that we don't bother posting the wedding banns at all. I want the wedding ceremony as soon as possible."

Usually, it was proper that the wedding banns announcing the upcoming marriage to be posted on the church door as well as at the castle and in the town for weeks before the wedding took place. That would give plenty of time in case someone decided to come forward and object to it. Well, after the rumors spread about Blaze, he didn't want to take a chance.

"I'll require your assistance as well," said another woman in the back of the cart whom Blaze recognized as the handmaid.

"Of course," said Blaze, not wanting to be rude. "Rosie, is it?" he asked, trying to remember her name as well as make small talk just to be polite.

"Posy," spat the woman, quickly releasing his arm once her feet touched the ground. "I'm here as handmaid to the Ladies Bonnel."

"I see." He really didn't expect this. Actually, he didn't think Lillith would be bringing her sister along either, and wondered why the girl was even here. Lord Bonnel didn't mention this in his missive. Blaze couldn't quite understand it. "Lillith, I didn't expect such a large traveling party."

"I thought my uncle sent you a missive announcing our arrival this morning," Lillith answered.

"He did. However, he must have forgotten to tell me I'd be entertaining so many."

"It is just temporary," she explained.

"It's kind of you to come, but I have servants here, Posy," Blake told the handmaid. "You can return to your castle because you're really not needed." Blaze saw his mother wandering over, hoping to hell she wasn't going to start trouble. Emery approached with her.

"Oh, I assure you, Lord Payne, my presence here is more than necessary," said Posy with her nose in the air.

"My lord, may I present the final wedding contract from Lord Bonnel in duplicate?" One of the guards who accompanied the women handed him the parchments. "You need to sign both copies to make the terms valid." The pageboy stood next to him with a feather pen and a bottle of ink.

"Of course, but I thought I already signed it," said Blaze. "Why more?"

"It's just a formality," said the guard. "For the records. Lord Bonnel already has signed them as well."

"My, he's anxious," said Blaze, taking the parchments, and unrolling one. "But not as anxious as me."

"Lord Bonnel likes to be quick and efficient," said the guard. "Just sign both at the bottom please."

Blaze already knew what the contract said since he'd read it earlier when he'd agreed to the proposal. He grabbed the feather pen and dipped it into the bottle of ink.

"Wait, Blaze. Before you sign those, we need to talk," said Lillith.

"I plan on talking for hours with you, Lilly, but just need to finalize the details first."

"Please, Blaze. Don't sign them."

"Now is not a good time for getting cold feet, Lilly." He signed them and handed one back to the guard. Then he rolled up the second parchment and handed it to Emery.

"Where would you like us to put the dowry, my lord?" asked the guard.

"Dowry." Blaze had almost forgotten about this. Of course, he would have married Lillith with no dowry involved, it didn't matter. All that was important to him was that she was about to become his wife. "In my solar will be fine. Here comes my steward now," he said, nodding as the man approached. "He will show you the way."

Lillith didn't like deceiving Blaze, and needed to let him know what was going on before things went any further. She had no idea what was in those contracts he just signed, but she didn't trust her uncle. That is why she had tried to stop him. Too late now. He wouldn't listen. Mayhap she just should have blurted out her information after all.

Blaze was going to be devastated when he found out the truth. Lillith saw the way he'd smiled at her. He didn't truly know who he'd agreed to marry. She could tell he still had feelings for her. If that was the case, this deception could bring about a battle between him and her uncle. That was the last thing she wanted to see.

"Sister, do you think he knows?" whispered Serena. "I mean . . . he didn't say anything about it."

"I'm sure he doesn't, but I'm going to tell him," said Lillith, planning on getting this over with as fast as possible. She didn't want to hurt Blaze, but someone had to tell him the truth.

"Tell me, what?" Blaze walked up behind her. His mother followed.

"Blaze, you scared me," said Lillith, spinning around and letting out a deep breath. Her hand went to her heart. He frowned.

"I've never scared you before, Lilly. What's going on with you?"

"Like I said, there is something I need to talk to you about."

"Why don't we all go inside to the great hall. It'll be more comfortable and a little more private there." He held out his arm for Lillith. Lillith's eyes darted over to her sister and they exchanged worried glances. "Lillith, if you're going to be my bride, it is customary to let me escort you. Why are you acting so odd? And by the way, why is your sister and handmaid here with you? It's really not necessary."

"Oh, it really is," she said, trying to gently lead into the information she was about to reveal to him.

"It's because they're deceiving you, Blaze," blurted out his mother. Lillith saw Blaze throw his mother a daggered look.

"Mother, I wasn't talking to you," Blaze said in a low voice. Lillith swore she saw his jaw twitch. "Stop trying to cause trouble." He placed Lillith's hand on his arm and started walking to the manor, taking her with him. Serena and Posy followed right behind them.

"Uh . . . Blaze, I'm afraid my uncle wasn't really clear about the terms in the betrothal contract," said Lillith.

"Clear? Oh, you mean about the date," he said, continuing to walk, placing his hand over Lillith's, as she clung to his arm. It felt damned good and almost made her want to cry. This should be her betrothal, not Serena's. Once again, life was taking a wicked turn for her and there was nothing she could do to stop it. "Don't worry, I'll take care of everything. I'll convince your uncle to let us marry sooner than the allotted time, I promise. We've waited far too long for this."

"Nay, I'm afraid that won't happen," she said, trying to figure out exactly how to say it.

"Why not?" he asked.

"Blaze, listen to me," said his mother, catching up to them. "My cards showed me that this arrangement isn't what you think it is."

"Enough with the cards, mother. Now hush up," Blaze warned her, looking at her from the corners of his eyes. "Stop trying to ruin this alliance."

"I'm doing no such thing," protested his mother. "All I'm saying is that the girl I saw in the cards that you're to marry has blond hair, not black."

"Oh!" gasped Lillith, realizing Blaze's mother had used some witchery to discover the truth. This wasn't at all the way Lillith wanted him to find out.

"My mother is just a little addled. Ignore her," said Blaze, forcing a chuckle. "She means nothing by it." They ascended the steps to the keep. He opened the door for her and they entered into the corridor, leading to the great hall.

It had been many years since Lillith stepped foot into Skull Manor. Unfortunately, it only looked spookier than she'd remembered it from her younger days. It got its name after a battle many years ago that left it burned, stark, and looking like a skull, with gaping holes in it that reminded people of a nose, eyes, and mouth. Of course, it no longer looked that way now.

Even though it was daytime, the manor was dark and cold. It was only a small holding, nothing that could compare to a castle. Its stone walls closed in around her, making her feel as if she couldn't breathe. It always seemed so dark, cold, musty, and lonely in here. That is why in the past she'd always suggest that she and Blaze spend time outdoors instead. She wondered how Blaze could even stand it living here.

A lone torch lit up the passageway, barely throwing enough light to see. The flame cast a shadow on the wall that looked like a laughing skull. A shiver ran through her body. Was this some kind of magic the witch brewed up? She hadn't known Blaze's mother had even returned to Skull Manor. The woman had always seemed odd to her, and they'd never really talked much. Now that Lillith knew Minerva was a witch, it scared her more than anything. Lillith didn't want to do anything to anger the woman.

If she did, she might end up cursed, crazy, and dead, just like her brother, Robert.

Minerva was already talking about having used her cards to see the future. Those cards were evil as far as Lillith was concerned. Once when she and Blaze were children, they tried to do their own reading. Lillith drew cards with horrible pictures on them, giving her nightmares for a month. Ever since then, she wanted nothing to do with them again.

"Just bring the dowry through here and to the room at the end of the hall," instructed Barnaby, directing Lillith's guard and page. Barnaby was the castle steward, and a man who had always been loyal to Blaze's family, as far as Lillith knew. However, she got the feeling that he had never approved of her in the past and still didn't. He gave her that look with one eye narrowed that said he didn't think Lillith was good enough for Blaze. Then again, she supposed it shouldn't matter since she wasn't the one marrying him anyway. Perhaps Barnaby would like Serena better.

"I didn't even ask what's in your dowry," said Blaze, bringing her to the great hall. The others followed.

"It's not," she answered.

"Not? Not what? You mean not what I'd expect?" He chuckled. "Don't worry about it, Lillith. I'd marry you even without a dowry. All that matters to me is that we're together again."

Oh, God, why was he making this so hard to tell him the truth? The last thing she wanted to do was to hurt him when he sounded so happy and excited about the betrothal.

"I've got your favorite meal prepared," he told her. "My cooks made venison in dill gravy with those tiny little onions you adore, cooked just the way you like it." Blaze escorted her up to the dais. "Your sister can sit with us if she wants, but the others will have to sit below the salt."

"Blaze, I'm not sure you're going to want me up here at all once I tell you what I have to say."

"Nonsense." He pulled out her chair for her. "I'm so happy right now that nothing you say could ever upset me."

"Don't bet on it," mumbled Lillith taking a seat.

Blaze was polite and helped Serena to get seated as well. His head guard, Emery whom Lillith remembered, sat next to Blaze. Next to Emery was Blaze's mother. Usually just the nobles sat at the dais. However, it didn't seem that Skull Manor had any nobles anymore besides Blaze and his mother. She figured all the knights must have left after the death of his father.

"Everyone, raise your cup," said Emery, standing up and holding his cup in the air. "Today is a special day. It is the day that the feud with the Bonnels has finally ended, because of a betrothal and very special alliance. I'd like us all to drink to Lord Blaze and his new bride-to-be."

"I agree," said Blaze, lifting his cup high as well. "My bride, please stand and join us in the toast."

Lillith looked over to Serena.

"What should I do?" Serena whispered.

"Come on, don't be shy. Stand up, so everyone can see you and drink in your beauty," Blaze said to Lillith.

"You'd better stand," Lillith whispered back to Serena.

"Nay!"

"Do it, Sister."

Looking like she was going to swoon, Serena slowly stood up, lifting her cup in the air with one shaking hand.

"Lillith, I said I wanted my bride-to-be to stand. Why are you still sitting?" asked Blaze softly. "And why in heaven's name is your sister standing instead of you?"

"I can't stand, Blaze," explained Lillith, feeling her nerves getting the best of her, knowing what was about to come. If he really was a warlock, there would be no telling what he might do if he thought they betrayed him. Which they had.

"Why not?" asked Blaze.

"Because," she said, letting out a deep breath and closing her eyes, not able to look at him when she said the words she dreaded more than anything in life right now. "You are not betrothed to me, Blaze. You have made an alliance to marry my sister, Serena."

Seven

"WHAT DID YOU SAY?" Blaze thought at first that he'd misheard Lillith and that she had said he was betrothed to her sister. Then, when he saw her eyes close and the tension on her face, he knew that he hadn't misheard a thing. Lillith twirled the end of her hair around her finger the way she always did when she was bothered deeply.

"She said you're marrying her sister, not her," said Emery, leaning closer to Blaze and speaking in a low voice.

"I heard what she said, you fool," said Blaze with a clenched jaw. Everyone watched from the filled trestle tables, all still holding their goblets of wine in the air. Blaze began to panic. "Lillith, what is going on?" He talked to her but kept his eyes out on the rest of the people. The smile remained on his face but it was far from real.

"I'm sorry, really I am," said Lillith. Tears formed in her eyes. "My uncle purposely didn't write Serena's name on the betrothal proposal, knowing you would think he meant me."

"Obviously. Now, tell me everything before I explode." Blaze looked directly at her now. She had opened her eyes and was staring up at him too. Sadness showed in her big blue orbs that seemed to change from the color of a summer's sky to that

70

of an approaching storm in a matter of seconds. It was evident that this deceitful act was not to her liking nor of her doing either. That should make Blaze feel better he supposed, but it didn't.

"Uncle Arthur . . . he really wants an alliance," she continued. "I mean, now that Father is gone and Uncle Arthur has no real qualms with you, he decided it would be a good thing to do."

"Did he also think it was a good idea to enter into an alliance with such deception?" asked Blaze, biting off his words. He felt so frustrated he was ready to shout, but tried to keep his voice down so the entire manor wouldn't hear his private conversation.

"Well, no," said Lillith. "I mean, I don't agree with his methods at all."

"I can't align with someone I don't trust."

"Blaze, to be fair, that is what alliances are for, aren't they? To bring enemies together."

Blaze shook his head, unable to believe this was happening to him. Just when he finally thought his troubles were behind him, now they were staring him in the face instead. "What your uncle did is not right at all."

"I believe my uncle only did it because he thought if he put Serena's name down on the contract, you might say no."

"And he would have been damned right about that."

"Oh," said Serena, holding a hand to her mouth, looking like she was about to cry.

"No disrespect to you, Lady Serena," Blaze told her. "I'm sure you'll make a wonderful wife to some man someday. Just not me."

Serena whimpered.

Lillith reached out and placed her hand over her sister's arm to try to calm her and then glared at him. "Blaze, you are scaring her. Now, please stop it. She did nothing wrong."

Blaze lowered his cup, staring down in anger at Lillith. "Nay, that was your uncle who did something worthy of starting not just another feud, but a battle this time. Possibly even a war."

"Stop exaggerating," she scoffed.

"Lillith, I didn't agree to marry your sister. I was led to believe I was agreeing to marry you."

"I saw the contract," Lillith told him. "It said Lady Bonnel. Why didn't you ask which one before you signed it?"

"I didn't think I needed to," he replied, now feeling like a fool. "Everyone knows we planned on marrying one day. We had a verbal agreement from our fathers. I won't go through with this wedding unless my betrothed is you, Lilly."

That only seemed to make Lillith even more upset. Especially since he called her Lilly. This was something that only he called her. It had always made her feel special in the past. Now, it seemed to make her feel miserable instead.

"My lord, everyone is waiting," said Emery under his breath, still holding his cup in the air and forcing a smile.

"Let them wait. I need this settled, and fast." Blaze banged his cup down on the table, waiting for answers and solutions to this newfound problem.

"I knew I shouldn't have stood up," said Serena in a meek voice, hurriedly sitting back down and keeping her eyes lowered.

"Lillith, you need to get your uncle to change the betrothal," he told her.

"H-he can't," she said, wiping a tear from her eye.

"Why not?" asked Blaze. "I want to marry you. Don't you want to marry me?"

"I – I – Oh, Blaze, don't you see? It doesn't matter what I want."

"Well, I think it does. I also don't see the problem. After all, your uncle never said which of you I was marrying. Therefore, I'll still be betrothed to a Lady Bonnel, just as the contract says."

Emery cleared his throat. When Blaze looked over at him, he pointed down at the final contract that Blaze had just signed for Lillith's guard before the man went back to Alderwood. Blaze had been so eager that he'd signed it without reading it. It was opened now. Emery had obviously read it. "Actually, my lord, I believe this is the final signed contract right here, and I hate to say that Serena's name is on it after all."

"What?" Blaze grabbed the contract, and held it up to inspect it. He didn't think he needed to read it since he knew what it said. But now, there, as plain as day, was Serena's name, not Lillith's. It no longer said he was marrying Lady Bonnel. Now it said Lady Serena Bonnel. The sneaky uncle of hers must have planned for this to happen. "Nay. This isn't right," he said, shaking his head. Being fooled once was unacceptable. Being fooled twice was an action worthy of starting a war over in his opinion. Blaze threw the parchment down on the table. "Lillith, I won't put up with this."

"But it's a binding contract, my lord," said Emery from behind him. "If you break it, the feud will never be ended."

Blaze thought about all the trouble they'd had over the past years involving the feud. His stable had been set on fire, and many of his crops had been burned by Henri Bonnel. To retaliate, Roger Payne had stolen a good number of the Bonnels' livestock, not to mention he also contaminated their moat with oil. That was only a precursor to the rumors each side spread about the other that kept deals from going through with other lords.

"You're right. I can't live with an ongoing feud any longer." Blaze brushed back his hair. "Nay, I'm not going to break the betrothal after all. I'm just going to change it. Just like Arthur Bonnel did. Now, Lillith, your uncle needs to replace Serena's name with your name on this parchment, and it needs to be done right away. The only Lady Bonnel I am marrying is you."

"I'm afraid that's not possible," Lillith squeaked out. He noticed the troubled look on her face, and wondered why she was fighting this suggestion.

"Why not?" he asked.

"Because Lady Lillith is already betrothed to someone else. Aren't you, my dear?" Minerva stood up and walked over to Blaze. "Son, you should have listened to me when I was trying to tell you what the cards warned me about earlier," she told him.

"Nay! This isn't true. It can't be." Blaze looked back at Lillith. "Tell me it isn't so. Are you really betrothed to someone else, Lilly?"

"I'm sorry, Blaze. My father betrothed me to Baron Edward Bancroft before he died," she answered. "The acceptance just came through and the contracts are signed."

"You're marrying a baron?" he asked, thinking now that mayhap he wasn't good enough for Lillith. After all, he wasn't even a knight. He hadn't thought titles meant so much to her, but obviously he was wrong.

"We are scheduled to marry as soon as he returns from campaigning overseas with the king."

"Bid the devil, this can't be happening," said Blaze through his teeth. "I've been tricked and I don't like it."

"I'm sorry, Blaze." Lillith got to her feet. "I don't blame you for being angry. You don't deserve this. I think it is best if my sister and I leave now. I'll talk to my uncle and explain to him how you feel. Come, sister. We will leave and Lord Blaze will never have to see us again."

"Nay, wait." Blaze said, reaching out and taking Lillith by the arm. "Don't leave. Please." It had been so long since he'd had Lillith near, and he didn't want it to end this way. Besides, if they went home now and told Arthur how he felt, another feud would be started.

Lillith slowly turned her head to look at his hand on her arm. Then her eyes drifted up to meet his. His mistake was looking directly into her eyes, because it only made him lose his heart to her again.

"I don't understand," she said softly. "Do you want the betrothal or not?"

"Nay. Aye. I mean . . . I'll handle negotiations with your uncle. In the meantime, I'd like you and your sister and your traveling party to stay here at Skull Manor. As my guests."

"Blaze, do you think that's a wise decision?" asked his mother, shooting daggers from her eyes at the girls.

"It's my decision, Mother, and you have no opinion in this matter. Lillith, will you stay?"

"Well, I don't know." Lillith looked at Serena and her sister shrugged. It was clear that neither of the girls knew exactly what to do. "I suppose we could stay for now." Lillith sat back down. "But you're not going to be able to change a thing, no matter what you think."

"We'll see," said Blaze, sitting back down feeling infuriated, exhausted and confused.

* * *

An hour later, Lillith closed the door to the bedchamber that she, Serena and Posy were sharing during their visit at Skull Manor.

"Well, I suppose that didn't go as badly as I thought it would," remarked Lillith, turning around to find her sister lying on her back on the bed. Her arm was thrown over her face. "I mean, Blaze did ask us to stay. That must mean he still has hope."

"I was sure I was going to swoon," said Serena, being dramatic as always. "I'm so glad you are here with me, Lillith, because that man scares me to no end."

"He's a warlock. He'd scare anyone. Just like that evil witch of a mother of his." Posy busied herself going through one of the trunks that held the girls' clothes. "Lady Serena, your gown is going to get wrinkled if you insist on lying in bed with it on. Mayhap you should change. You'll look terrible when you go out to the courtyard this afternoon to mingle with Lord Blaze's household."

"Mingle?" Serena shot up in bed. "I'm not going to mingle. I am going to stay right here in this chamber where I'm safe, until we find a way to break the betrothal and go home. I can't wait to get out of here before those witches curse me or kill me, like what happened to our brother and father."

"Stop it, Serena. You are just scaring yourself," said Lillith, feeling the weight of the world on her shoulders. "Robert and

Father were not cursed by anyone. I'm sure their deaths were purely accidental."

"How can you say that?" asked Posy. "Your brother went mad and jumped off a cliff because of Lord Blaze's mother."

"We don't know that," said Lillith. "It could just all be rumors."

"He's dead" said Serena. "That must mean something to you."

"No one ever found his body," said Lillith, part of her wanting to protect the Paynes, though right now she wasn't sure why.

"There were eye witnesses that heard him making odd noises atop that cliff, just before he disappeared," said Posy. "You know as well as anyone that not even his body survived the curse. They only found his hat floating in the sea."

"Lillith, I want to go home right now." Serena's entire body started shaking.

"Stop it, Posy. Stop it, both of you." Lillith walked over to the bed and sat down and put her arm around her sister. "You are both scaring yourselves. I don't believe any of these stories are true. Blaze has always been like part of our family."

"He might have been acting that way just to get close to us to kill us," said Serena. "We can't trust him."

The shutter from the window blew opened and banged against the wall, and then slammed shut, causing them all to jump and scream. Lillith's heart lodged in her throat. All this talk was making her confused about Blaze and his family and scaring her as well, although she wouldn't admit it to her sister and handmaid.

"Lady Lillith, I have to agree with your sister on this one," said Posy slamming shut the trunk and putting her hands on her hips. "After all, you heard Minerva telling Blaze something about those devil cards she reads. There is no telling what these people are capable of doing. I suggest we all sleep with one eye open."

"This place is scary," said Serena slowly taking in their surroundings.

Lillith had to agree with her on that. The room was dark and cold. Everything was covered with cobwebs. It looked like no one had occupied this room in a very long time. The rushes on the floor were dirty, and smelled like dust. The room was stark of furniture. Besides the bed, there was a small table and chairs but that was it, except for their trunks stacked up against the wall.

"I keep thinking some ghost is going to jump out at me, coming from inside the wall." Serena clung tighter to Lillith.

"That's nonsense. The manor just needs a woman's touch. And a little cleaning." Lillith forced a smile. "Blaze's mother was gone for five years so I'm sure that is why this place isn't better kept."

"He has servants for that, doesn't he?" asked Posy.

"Well, mayhap he needs better ones," she mumbled, for lack of a better answer. "The manor might be a little dark and dingy, but I'm sure all it needs is some fresh air and sunshine." Lillith walked over to the window and opened the shutters, glancing down into the courtyard. There, she saw Blaze and his mother walking together, heading toward the front gate.

"What are you looking at?" asked Posy, coming up behind her. "Oh, good. The witches are leaving the manor."

"At least we can relax now," said Serena with a deep sigh, falling on her back again and throwing her arm over her face once more.

"Relax? I think we should look for that dagger Milo said he saw on the ground next to your father," said Posy. "If we find it here at the manor, we'll know it was Blaze's. That will prove Milo really did see him at the site of your father's death."

"What?" asked Lillith. "That wouldn't mean a thing. You two are acting like Father was murdered. You heard what Uncle Arthur said. Father was drunk and went hunting and fell off his horse onto his own blade."

"Uh huh," said Posy in a tone that said she thought Lillith was a fool.

"Posy's right, Lillith." Serena sat up and hurriedly scooted off the bed. "We need answers. You know this manor better than anyone since you came here to play when you were a child. Go now. Sneak into Blaze's solar and see what you can find out. If nothing else, I'm sure there will be evidence of them being witches and warlocks. If you find something, we might be able to convince Uncle Arthur to break the betrothal after all."

"And then we can get out of here and go back home." Posy sat down on the bed next to Serena, putting her arm around the girl's shoulders.

"I'll do no such thing," Lillith retorted. "We have no right to go through Lord Blaze's things." The biggest reason she fought this suggestion was because she knew damned well that dagger was his but didn't want the others to know.

"Aren't you even a little curious about Blaze possibly being a warlock?" asked Posy.

"He's not," Lillith answered quickly, shaking her head. Her heart went out to Blaze. It seemed like everyone was against him, and she wanted to be that one person who would defend him. Even if she was a little skeptical and angrier than hell that he'd lied to her about the warlock issue, part of her still loved him. She had been listening for too many years to her father and his opinions about the Paynes. Blaze was right. She did carry her late father's attitudes and beliefs and that didn't sit right with her. She had never let anyone sway her decisions. What was happening to her? She didn't want to see anything bad happen to Blaze or his family.

"Sister, his mother is a witch and everyone knows it," said Serena. "You heard her talking about those cards she reads. Didn't you ever know about it?"

"Me?" Lillith didn't want to admit that she had known about the cards. She also didn't want to be part of this conversation any longer. Just needing to get away from Posy and Serena, she agreed to the task after all.

"Sister?" asked Serena, waiting for her answer.

"Fine," she said, throwing her arms up in the air. "I will sneak into Blaze's solar to find out what I can. But I'm only agreeing to this because you two are scared of something that doesn't even exist. I'm going to prove it to you once and for all that Blaze is naught but a man. A normal man."

"Thank you," said Serena, giving Lillith a kiss on the cheek.

Lillith sneaked down the corridor and into Blaze's room, managing to get in without anyone seeing her. She stopped for a moment and looked around his private quarters. It was really no different than what she remembered from when she was fifteen. She and Blaze had been starting to see each other as more than just friends, but had never done anything about it. Then, while hiding from his mother one day after they had accidentally broken one of her favorite vases, Blaze had brought Lillith here. This is where they'd shared their first kiss.

His big bed still sat on the far side of the room, and she was instantly drawn to it. The purple velvet curtains that hung from iron rings enclosing the bed were open and tied back, just the way she'd remembered. With one missing, of course. Lillith smiled, running her hand down the soft velvet, liking the way it felt. She had always loved the color purple and had been so surprised to find out that Blaze liked purple too. He actually used one of the bedcurtains to have a gown made out of it for Lillith for her birthday. She'd been wearing that gown when they'd kissed.

It was right here at the side of the bed where Blaze had wrapped his arms around her and pulled her close to him. Then he'd gently placed his mouth on hers. Lillith hadn't known anything about kissing, never having experienced it before. It was the moment that changed her life. It was then that their relationship moved from just friendship to something so much more. The kiss was fast and simple, but it had been so sensual, exciting, and powerful, that it had frightened Lillith a little.

Blaze had a look in his eyes that said he wanted to be intimate. Since they'd been standing at the side of his bed, Lillith's mind went wild with thoughts of them being atop it together. She knew those thoughts were improper, and was ashamed of herself for even thinking about it. So, instead of kissing him a second time, or giving things a chance to turn to anything else, Lillith ran for home.

Sadly, that was the last she'd seen of him before the feud began between their families. Once that happened, everything changed between them, and the spark that had been ignited that day was quickly doused.

Lillith ran her fingers up and down the carved wooden spindle of the bed, wondering if that kiss had affected Blaze as much as it had her. He must have liked it. After all, he was the one who so boldly kissed her again after not seeing each other for all these years. Sadly, instead of enjoying it, Lillith had slapped him and sent him away, ending it once more. A pain shot through her heart thinking about it. It hurt her to do it, but once again, she had been afraid. All this talk about him being a warlock and cursing or killing members of her family had just been too much for her to bear.

Even if Blaze wasn't what the rumors said he was, they still couldn't be together. He was betrothed to her sister now and Lillith was going to marry a baron. It should make her happy she supposed, that both she and Serena would be taken care of. Instead, it made her sad. Things were all wrong, and there was nothing she could do to change it.

As Lillith stood there reminiscing about the past, she didn't even hear the sound of the door opening behind her.

"Lillith? What are you doing?"

She jumped in surprise and spun around to see Blaze standing there with the man who worked in the stables.

"Blaze," she said, lost for words. She giggled nervously, trying to think of something believable to say.

"Thank you, Orvyn, just put it down over there and you may go."

"Of course, my lord." Orvyn's eyes fastened to Lillith as he placed a blanket and saddle down on the floor. "Are you sure you don't want me to fix the stitching on the saddle, my lord?"

"Nay. I enjoy doing things like that myself, but thank you."

"Aye, my lord." Orvyn looked at Lillith once more and headed for the door.

"Orvyn?" said Blaze, stopping the man in his tracks. "I'd appreciate it if you kept quiet about what you saw here."

"I didn't see anything but Lady Lillith, my lord. It's not like you've done anything wrong. I mean, other than she's the sister of the girl you're marrying, yet she is the one awaiting you in your sleeping quarters."

"For your trouble," said Blaze, handing the man a coin.

"Why, thank you, my lord," said Orvyn, eagerly taking the coin and bowing. Then he quickly left the room.

Blaze closed the door and turned back to Lillith.

When he did, he noticed Lillith becoming very fidgety all of a sudden.

"What are you doing in my solar?" he asked, slowly strolling across the floor toward her.

"I – I was looking for you, Blaze." Her eyes darted in one direction and then the other, and he saw her reaching for her dagger at her side.

"Really. Whatever for?" In two more long strides, he was standing in front of her, so close that he could reach out and touch her.

"I needed to talk to you."

"With a dagger pointed at my heart?" He grabbed her wrist and ripped the blade away from her. "What is going on with you?"

"I'm sorry."

"For what?" He slipped her dagger into the sheath at her side and then reached over her and leaned his arm on the bed spindle. This made their faces close enough to kiss. She ducked underneath his arm and scurried across the room. That told him that whatever the reason for her being here, she hadn't come to him for intimate purposes. Not that he thought she would, since he was betrothed to her sister and she was promised to another man.

Still, Blaze hadn't lost hope that mayhap Lillith still had feelings for him.

"I'm sorry about everything." Lillith sat down on a chair, and fidgeted with the candle on top of the table. "I mean, the feud, and the betrothal, of course. It wasn't my idea that things turned out like this."

"What was your idea?" he asked, walking up behind her. "By the way, you never told me why you came with your sister to Skull Manor."

He gently placed a hand on her shoulder from behind and felt her body immediately stiffen.

"I'm here to protect her," she said, surprising him with her answer.

"Protect her?" He chuckled. "From what? Or should I say whom?"

"She's afraid of you, Blaze. She thinks you're a warlock and doesn't want to be near you." She looked up with wide blue eyes, blinking twice in succession.

His fingers slowly slid off her shoulder. "Is that what you think, too?"

She let out a sigh and stood up and turned to face him. "Honestly, I'm not sure what to think anymore."

"What does that mean?" Blaze crossed his arms over his chest.

"It means I know your mother reads futures with cards and has some strange ways about her."

"That's my mother. Not me."

"And then there are a lot of rumors about you and your family."

"There will always be rumors and gossip in life. You need to learn not to listen to it, or you're no better than those who are spreading the lies."

"Some people even think you had something to do with my father's death."

"What?" he gasped. "I can't believe I'm even hearing this out of your mouth."

"I didn't say I believed it."

"But yet, you're here in my solar poking around. That tells me you don't trust me. You're looking for something. What is it?"

"What makes you think I'm not here looking for another kiss?" Her eyes flashed up to him, drawing him in. He never could stay angry at her when she looked at him in that manner. It was a cross between a playful, flirting action, and one that told him she needed to be hugged. She was also giving him that cute little pout again that drove him mad.

"If you were truly here for a kiss, you wouldn't have moved away from me when we were over by the bed." He moved away from her before he was tempted to touch her soft skin again.

"Mayhap I was playing hard to get." She followed him across the room, winding the end of her long locks around her fingers. He knew Lillith well enough that she only did that when she was extremely nervous.

"Lilly, I don't know what this game is you're playing with me, but I don't like it. And I sure as hell don't believe it, either."

Her slight grin turned into a frown. "All right, so I wasn't in here for a kiss," she finally admitted. "Do you want to hear the truth?"

"Yes. I do. I thought we never expected anything but the truth from each other, sweetheart. That's what made our friendship so strong through the years."

"You're right. You at least deserve that," she said, looking down and to the side when she told him, rather than looking directly into his eyes. "If you must know, I am in here looking for a dagger with moons and stars on it. The hilt is also carved into a skull. It's the dagger your mother gave you for your birthday one year. I remember it."

"I see." He slowly unfolded his arms and went over to a trunk and popped it open. He dug down into it and then held up something shiny. "Do you mean this?"

"Oh!" she gasped, holding her hand over her mouth when she saw the dagger.

Blaze walked over and held it out for her to take. She shook her head and backed away. "This is what you were looking for, isn't it?"

"I – I – Blaze, that is the dagger that Milo said he saw on the ground next to my father's body. Isn't it?"

"Yes, it is," he told her, not even trying to conceal the fact.

Her gaze slowly went from the dagger to his face. He saw fear in her eyes, and that was something he never wanted to witness. Now, she was afraid of him just like the rest of them.

"Milo said he saw a man in a cloak bending over my father and touching his face. And that the dagger was there and it had blood on it."

He hesitated, not wanting to admit it, but finally told her what happened. He didn't want to lie to her, especially after he made such a fuss that she was honest with him.

"Yes, that was me," he said tossing the dagger down atop the wooden table, not even trying to conceal the fact he'd been there.

"So did you – did you curse and kill my father?" The fear in her eyes as well as the anger was too much for him to bear. The woman he loved looked at him in disgust, and it didn't feel good at all.

He pulled out a chair and sat down, rubbing his hands over his face and letting out a whoosh of air from his mouth. Why did he feel like he was living in hell? When would it ever end?

"Let me explain, Lilly. I came across your father lying on the ground when I was out on one of my hunting trips. I touched your father's neck to determine that he was already dead and had no pulse. So I closed his eyes."

"Milo said he saw someone but they ran when he showed up. He said there was a blade on the ground next to my father with blood on it. It had moons and stars on the hilt and a skull carved into the top. He was scared and ran for help. When he returned with the others, the man and the dagger were gone."

"I told you, I was hunting. Of course, my blade had blood on it, but it wasn't from Henri. He fell on his own blade, not mine. I dropped it when I heard someone coming."

"You left my father there?"

"I didn't flee, if that's what you mean. I heard someone coming and knew I'd be blamed for your father's death. I have had enough trouble and didn't need more. I stepped behind a tree and watched. That's when I realized I'd dropped my dagger. So when the boy ran for help, I retrieved my dagger. Lilly, I'm sorry, but your father was dead when I got there. He smelled strongly from alcohol. My guess is that he was well in his cups and never should have been atop a horse. Don't you see? There was nothing I could do to help him."

"Oh," she answered, not saying anything more.

"You believe me, don't you?" It hurt him to think that she didn't trust him anymore.

"I suppose I do. I mean, yes. But what about the rumors of your family being witches?"

"Aaaah," he groaned and stood up and shook his head. He couldn't go on like this, keeping secrets from Lilly. "Yes. It's true. Partially."

"I-it is?" She looked scared again.

"It is," he said, standing in front of her now.

She sank atop a chair. "Blaze? You never told me this. We were so close and yet you lied?"

He knelt down in front of her and took her hands in his. "Lilly, I didn't lie. Not really. I'm sorry I kept it from you, but I didn't think you'd understand."

"Well, I don't."

"It's not what you think. I mean, my mother is called a witch but she's not evil."

"What about you?" Her hands were in fists beneath his, but he didn't pull away.

"I'm more like my father. He was . . . normal."

"So you don't partake in any of those things that your mother does?"

"I do once in a while, but it's really not me. I only participated to make my mother happy. So, no, I'm not a warlock. I mean, not really."

"I've got to go." She stood up quickly, almost knocking him over.

"Wait," he called out. "I want you to know that my family is really no different from you and your family."

"What?" She spun around. "How can you say that? We're Catholic."

"And so was my father. It's all right to be whatever you want to be. Why should anyone force their beliefs on others? And why are we judged by our decisions?"

"It's just the way it is, Blaze," she answered, shaking her head. Lillith slowly walked over to him, tilting her head and looking at him from the corners of her eyes. "Did you ever use a spell on me to get me to like you?"

"What? Nay!" He shot to his feet. "I wish you would just give me a chance to show you what we do without judging us."

"What? What is it you do?"

"I can't explain, but I can show you. Give me that chance, Lilly. At least give me that since soon you will be married to the baron and my chances of ever making you my wife are over."

"I – I don't know," she said, seeming to contemplate the suggestion. "What about your betrothal to my sister?"

"What about it?"

"Are you going to marry her?"

"I've signed an agreement. I don't like it since I was tricked, but if I can't have you, then what other choice do I have?"

"Do you swear that you and your family don't practice dark magic and control people's minds?"

"I swear it," he said, taking her hands in his. "Just give me another chance, my Lilly Bee. I want you to think good thoughts about me when you're raising a family with the baron. I want your memories of me to be fond ones, not bad."

"Oh, Blaze," she said, starting to cry. "Everything has been so difficult lately. All I want is for life to be carefree and simple again. The way it used to be."

He didn't ask, he just pulled her into his embrace. She gently laid her face against his chest. "I am here for you, Lilly," he said softly, kissing the top of her head and holding her shaking body against his. She smelled fresh, like the sweet morning dew. Her hair was soft like the gossamer wings of a butterfly, and he couldn't get his fill.

Blaze held her, knowing it might be the last chance he'd ever have to do so. He wanted to be her protector, not the one who scared her. That's the way it should be. The way he'd always meant it to be. He wanted to keep her safe and happy. That was all that mattered, even if he had to sacrifice his own happiness to do it. But never did he ever want the person he had to protect her from to be himself.

"Blaze, what's taking you so long?" Minerva walked into the room and stopped in her tracks when she saw Lillith in his embrace. Lillith sniffled and pushed away, wiping a tear away with the back of her hand. "What's this?" asked the woman in a haughty tone.

"Hello, Lady Minerva," said Lillith, standing straighter. "I was just leaving." She brushed past the woman, making a beeline for the door.

"Lillith? Aren't you forgetting something?" Blaze's eyes flashed over to the dagger on the table. He wanted to see what she would do. If she brought it back to her uncle, it would mean she didn't believe him or trust him. If she left it, he would know that mayhap he could get her to forgive him after all.

"Nay. I don't believe so," she said, trying to sound cheery. "Goodbye." Then she was gone, leaving Blaze standing there with his mother.

"What was that all about?" asked Minerva with a frown. She was back to looking at him with narrowed eyes again in a suspicious manner. "Blaze, did something happen between you and that girl?"

"Her name is Lillith, Mother. And nay, nothing happened in the way you mean. Although, I must say I wouldn't have minded if it had."

"She's not your betrothed, Blaze. You're to marry her sister, unless you've already forgotten."

"Don't remind me." He headed over and picked up the dagger, running a hand over it in thought.

"What's that doing out?" she asked. "I thought I told you to hide it, before it linked you somehow to Lord Bonnel's death."

"Lillith was looking for it," he told her, walking back to the trunk and placing it back inside.

"Why? What did you tell her?"

"I told her the truth."

His mother's eyes opened wide. "The truth? About what?"

"About everything. I am done lying to the woman I love."

"Blaze Payne, I warn you, this will come back to haunt you someday."

"The only thing haunting me is my heart, Mother. I'm afraid I'm in love with Lilly but I can't marry her. I'm betrothed to her sister, but I'm not sure I can marry her either."

"Why not?"

"Because it would hurt too much. For both of us," he said.

"Blaze, you signed a contract. Besides, you heard Lillith. She is betrothed to a baron now. If you go around breaking your word, you'll be fighting other lords the rest of your life."

"I know. And if I do nothing to try to get Lilly back, I'll regret it until the day I die. I lose either way, don't I?"

"What are you going to do?"

"I'm not sure. But one thing I do know is that I'm going to prolong the wedding and keep Lilly here as long as possible. Because every minute I spend with her will be a memory that will have to last me for the rest of my life."

Eight

"SISTER, did you find any evidence in Blaze's solar?" Serena ran across the room to meet Lillith at the door when she returned to their chamber. "Did you find that dagger or some things used by witches?"

"Yes, did you?" asked Posy curiously, straightening out the blankets on the bed.

"I – nay. I have nothing to report. Blaze walked in before I had time to leave," she said. "I made excuses and tried to get out of there quickly before he became suspicious."

"Why did you tell him you were there?" Posy looked over as she slowly continued to fold a blanket. "I mean, I'd think your being in his chamber was already suspicious enough."

"It doesn't matter. We were friends for a long time, so I'm sure he thinks nothing of it." Lillith was in no hurry to share information with these two. They despised Blaze and his family and she didn't want to add fuel to the fire. She certainly couldn't come out and tell them Blaze more or less admitted he was a warlock.

What she needed was to get away and clear her head. She'd just learned a lot of shocking information and wasn't sure what to think about any of it.

"I think I'll go for a quick ride in the woods," said Lillith, trying to change the subject. "I mean, It's such a nice day and all."

"Good idea. I'll come with you," said Serena, eager to leave the manor. "Mayhap we can stop back home and see Mother."

Lillith realized her sister didn't feel comfortable at Skull Manor, but she didn't want anyone along with her right now. She also didn't want Posy or Serena to tell Arthur that Blaze knew of the betrothal deception and wasn't happy about it. That was trouble waiting to happen.

"Nay, you and Posy need to stay here and help Blaze and his mother make the plans for your wedding," Lillith told them.

"What?" Serena's head snapped up. "I'm not marrying him, Lillith. You've got to help me get out of this betrothal."

"I won't be gone long," promised Lillith, walking out into the corridor.

Lillith hurried out to the stable, hoping her sister wouldn't follow. She entered the stable and went directly to the stall that held the horse they'd used to pull the wagon. Her guards had already left on their horses, and she didn't have her own horse from Alderwood Castle here. Now, she regretted not bringing it with her. This horse wasn't fast enough to outrun a snail. It was also not good for riding, but used mainly for pulling the wagon.

She walked to the adjoining stall and entered, seeing one of Blaze's horses that she figured she would use instead.

"Nice girl," she said, patting the horse's flank. She decided to saddle and borrow it, and return it when she was done. She was sure Blaze wouldn't mind. Lillith knew how to ride astride, so any of the saddles would do.

"Lady Lillith? Is that you?"

A boy poked his head up from sleeping in the hay. "Where are you going?"

"Milo?" Her heart sank when she saw her page walking over to join her. "I'll be right back. I'm just going for a short ride, that's all."

"Then I'll come with you," the boy offered. "You shouldn't go out unescorted."

"You're just a page. What could you possibly even do to protect me?" she said in aggravation.

"I've been practicing with my weapons and hope to be a squire someday." Milo put his hand on his waist, then realized he wasn't even wearing his weapon belt. He hurried back to the sleeping spot, picked up his belt with weapons, and strapped it around him. "I'll be able to protect you, my lady. Honest, I will."

"Oh, Milo, I don't think so."

The look of disappointment in his eyes made her want to build him up instead of bring him down. He was a boy with a dream and that was important. She needed to boost the boy's confidence to keep that dream alive, even if it never came true. Lillith realized that everyone needed something to look forward to in life. Milo had been practicing hard, hoping for nothing more than to actually become a squire someday. As much as she didn't want him along, she also didn't want to hurt him either.

"Well, mayhap it would be good to have a man along," she answered, watching a smile spread across his face when she called him a man.

His eyes sparkled and he stood up straighter. "I'll saddle the horse from our wagon right away."

"You do that," she said, seeing a saddle and picking it up to use on the horse she would be using.

"That's Lord Blaze's horse, my lady." Orvyn walked into the stables and hurried toward her. "What are you doing with it?"

Right now, Lillith felt like screaming. She was trying to sneak out of there and it was becoming a public affair. With Orvyn there too, now it would be impossible to leave in secret. Orvyn was Blaze's stablemaster. She was sure that he wasn't about to let her take one of Blaze's horses without his lord's permission.

"Lord Blaze knows about it," said Milo, surprising her. "Besides, I'm escorting her and will make certain that no harm comes to her or the horse."

"Really?" asked Orvyn. "Funny, but I just saw my lord in his solar, and you were there too, my lady."

"You were?" Milo's head snapped around in curiosity.

"Yes," continued Orvyn. "And Lord Blaze didn't mention that anyone would be borrowing his horse for a ride," he said to Lillith.

"I don't have my horse with me, and I'm sure Lord Blaze wouldn't mind. I'll bring it right back," said Lillith, flashing him one of her best smiles.

"Weeeeell, mayhap it would be all right. After all, I know you and Lord Blaze go way back," said the man, smiling back at her.

"Why were you in Lord Blaze's solar?" asked Milo.

Lillith cringed, but did not answer.

"This saddle is heavy," said Lillith looking over to Orvyn, trying to act helpless even though she was far from needing his assistance.

"That's my job, my lady. Let me do it for you." The stable-master reached out for it.

"Thank you. Orvyn, is it?"

"Yes, that's my name," he said, saddling and preparing the horse for her after all.

Lillith kept changing the subject and engaging the man in small talk, hoping he'd forget she was stealing a horse.

"You seem to know a lot about what goes on around here," said Lillith.

"Aye, I see and hear everything, my lady. Nothing escapes my notice."

"Then I suppose you know all about the day that my father died."

Orvyn became suddenly silent. "I'm sorry for your loss, my lady. It was an unfortunate accident indeed."

"I saw a man bending over Lord Bonnel but he disappeared," Milo told him. "So did the dagger that was next to Lord Bonnel on the ground."

Lillith cringed again. Why had she said this with Milo right here? She wasn't thinking with a clear head. She'd been trying to change the subject, but now the conversation took a completely different direction than she'd intended for it to go.

"Who did you see?" Orvyn asked Milo.

"I don't know. I never saw his face," answered the boy.

"Well, what kind of dagger was it?" Orvyn was good at asking questions and getting answers.

"It was ornate," said Milo, more than happy to share his information with the most talkative person at Skull Manor. "It had witchy things on it. Moons and stars and a skull carved into the hilt. Have you seen a dagger like that around here?"

"Well, that does sound a lot like Lord Blaze's dagger. I've seen it with him once or twice, but not for a while now," Orvyn answered.

This only made Lillith more uncomfortable than she already was. The last thing she wanted to do was to make everyone suspicious about Blaze. It was bad enough that everyone feared him. She didn't want them calling him a murderer now too.

"Milo, I'm ready to go," she said, mounting the horse. "I want to make this a fast trip. I need to get back to help with the planning of my sister's wedding."

"Is Lady Serena really going to marry the warlock?" asked Milo, faking a shiver.

"You know as well as anyone that my uncle made the betrothal to end the feud," Lillith answered, mounting the horse.

"It is odd that the Bonnels and the Paynes have been feuding for so long and now all of a sudden there's going to be a wedding," commented Orvyn, digging for more information. She needed to leave right now before she accidentally said anything else that would put Blaze in a bad light.

"Well, that's how alliances are usually formed, aren't they?" she asked, directing her horse out of the stall. She took off at a gallop with Milo right behind her. Lillith rode fast, heading for the woods, not wanting to think about Blaze and his kisses or his dagger anymore. Besides that, she really didn't want to think about Blaze marrying her sister. That bothered her even more than the fact he'd never told her about his family secrets.

Serena could never make Blaze happy, she decided. Serena would probably never even want to get close enough to Blaze to share a kiss. Blaze was a good kisser. Lillith wondered if she'd feel the same kind of excitement when the baron kissed her someday. Damn, why was she thinking about Blaze's kisses again? Her thoughts were running wild.

"Lady Lillith, wait for me," called out Milo, causing her to finally slow down. "This horse is too slow, but what's the big hurry?"

"I just feel like riding fast, that's all." She had gone deep into the woods, not even paying attention to where she was headed. The area around her didn't seem familiar anymore. They were in the forest surrounding Skull Manor.

"Look, my lady. What's that?" Milo rode up, pointing through the trees.

When Lillith looked where he pointed, she was able to see tall standing stones forming a circle up ahead in a small clearing. She directed her horse toward it, stopping just outside the circle when she realized exactly where she was. It was a witches' circle. She remembered now, years ago, having seen it. She was racing Blaze atop their horses and ended up here. She had asked him about it, but he had told her it wasn't important. She hadn't thought anything of it and actually forgot all about it.

She realized now that Blaze had been lying to her for even longer than she had thought. Why hadn't he just come out and told her?

"It looks like someone is going to have a bonfire here," said Milo, pointing from atop his horse to the pyre of sticks and logs stacked up in the center of the stone circle. "I'll bet it's where those witches do their spells. Especially since it is so close to All Hallows' Eve. I've heard it said they call it Samhain. It is also said that's the time when the veil between the two worlds is the thinnest and the dead can come back to roam the earth."

Lillith had heard those stories too and they had only managed to frighten her. She surveyed the stone circle, not seeing anything but nature. This didn't seem frightening at all.

"Milo, that's all nonsense. Those are just stories made up to scare the children on All Hallows' Eve."

"I don't think so," he said, shaking his head. His eyes were still fastened on the stone circle. "We should go tell your uncle about this. It's important. This proves the Paynes are witches."

"I'm sure this is naught but an old structure where hunters warmed themselves for the night."

"Nay. It's a place where witches hold their ceremonies. I know it is." Milo wouldn't let up. Lillith now regretted bringing him along.

"Milo, I think it's best we leave here now. It would be better if you didn't say anything about this. My sister and handmaid are at Skull Manor and are already spooked. Plus, I don't want my uncle causing trouble for the Paynes. We are trying to make an alliance, not start another feud."

"I understand," he said with a slight nod. "I think the road is back that way," he told her, nodding with his head. "Lady Lillith, we are not that far from Alderwood Castle. Mayhap you could stop back there for your horse."

Lillith knew exactly why Milo wanted to go back to the castle. He wanted to tell her uncle everything. Well, she couldn't let him do that right now. She needed more time to figure things out. Actually, she wanted more time to spend with Blaze before she had to marry a man she didn't want or love. Lillith was not going to let Milo ruin that for her.

* * *

Blaze rode through the woods with the wind in his hair, trying to track down Lillith. When Orvyn told him that she was out riding, he knew it meant trouble. He had to stop her before she returned to her uncle and told him all his secrets. If she did that, he was sure Lord Arthur would find a way to blame him for Lord Henri's death. He couldn't have ill-talk and accusations about him now. He was so close to being accepted as a knight by the earl that he didn't want anything to ruin his chances. Marrying Serena was not what he wanted, but still it would be his ticket to finally getting the title he coveted.

His raven led the way, and Blaze followed. The bird had always seemed to be able to read his mind and know what Blaze wanted.

Finally, he spotted Lillith and her page just up ahead. Unfortunately, they were somewhere they shouldn't be. This was bad. Really bad. They were right outside of the stone circle.

"Damn," he mumbled, knowing this was only going to make things worse for him. His mother and some of 'their kind' had been preparing for the Samhain festival that was always held here in the center of the standing stones. "Lillith," he called out, getting her attention. His raven settled itself atop one of the tall stones.

"Blaze?" he heard her say in surprise. He directed his horse up to them. "What are you doing here?" asked Lillith. "Are you following me?"

"Orvyn told me you went out riding and I didn't feel it was safe for you to be alone."

"I'm not alone. I've got Milo with me, as you can see." She nodded to the page. When Blaze glanced at the boy, Milo quickly looked the other way.

"Yes. I see. But I don't think you need the task of protecting him as well if you run across any ruffians." That got Milo to look directly at him.

"I'm here to protect her, my lord." Milo sounded extremely insulted. "I have training with weapons, and someday I'm going to be a squire."

"Of course, you are," he mumbled. "Lillith, let me escort you back to the manor."

"There's really no need for that," said Lillith.

"We're stopping at Alderwood Castle before we head back," announced the boy.

"You are?" He looked over at Lillith and raised a brow. "Whatever for?"

"Nay, we are not," said Lillith, glaring at Milo. "We were just headed back to Skull Manor."

They heard thunder and he looked up at the sky that was darkening quickly.

"It's going to storm," said Blaze. "I suggest we hurry before we get wet."

"Yes, I agree," said Lillith.

"This horse couldn't hurry if it sat on a nest of ants," complained Milo, turning his steed around.

"Milo, switch horses with Lady Lillith and ride back to the manor quickly before it rains."

"What about Lady Lillith?" asked the boy. "She'll get drenched if she has to ride this broken-down old nag."

"I'll ride with Lady Bonnel. Don't worry about it," said Blaze.

"My lord?" said Lillith, looking up in surprise.

"You'll ride with me," he said. "I can keep you dry under my cloak. We'll bring the slow horse back with us. Go on, Milo," ordered Blaze.

"My lady?" Milo looked over to Lillith in question as the rain started to come down faster now.

"Go on, Milo. Do as Lord Payne says." Lillith dismounted, and traded horses with Milo and the boy left them.

"Let me help you up, my lady." Blaze reached down and pulled Lillith up onto the horse, settling her in front of him. He wrapped his arms as well as his cloak around her, trying to shelter her from the rain.

"I have the distinct feeling you wanted to be alone with me," she told him as he turned the horse and headed in the opposite direction from the manor. "Blaze, why are we going this way? It isn't the way back to the manor is it?"

"Nay, but it is the way to Alderwood Castle."

"What?" she squeaked. "We're not going there."

"Why not?" asked Blaze.

"You're going to confront my uncle about the trick he played on you, aren't you?"

"Actually, no. I realized it no longer matters."

"It doesn't?"

"Lilly, I know now that I can't have you. So, I'll just have to settle for your sister instead."

"Really? You will?" This seemed to shock her.

"I want to be part of your family, and if this is the only way to do it, then so be it. I want to thank Arthur personally for suggesting the alliance that will stop the feud and bring our families back together again."

Blaze actually wanted to try to talk Arthur into breaking the betrothal and letting him marry Lillith instead. She didn't need to know that right now. If she really cared for him, and he thought she did, mayhap she'd help him. If Blaze couldn't convince Arthur, mayhap Lillith could.

Nine

LILLITH FELT furious with Blaze by the time they arrived at Alderwood Castle. The last thing she wanted right now was to bring him inside her home. Everyone was going to be alarmed that he was there. She could only hope no one would try to kill him.

"It's Lady Lillith," called out one of the guards from the battlements as they rode over the drawbridge and into the courtyard. The rain continued to soak them.

"My lady," said the stableboy running up to greet them. "May I take your horse?"

"Nay," she said. "We're not staying."

"Aye, you may." Blaze dismounted and then helped Lillith to the ground. "Can you tell me where to find Lady Lillith's uncle?"

"Blaze, no," she said in a mere whisper, not able to believe he was really going through with this.

"Lord Arthur is in the great hall feasting with Lady Beatrice and his knights," said the boy.

"Thank you." Blaze took her hand guided her toward the great hall.

"Blaze, stop this. I don't know what kind of game you're playing, but I don't like it."

He stopped in his tracks, looking at her with a stone-like face.

"Me playing a game? I think it is your family playing a game at my expense."

"Let's just leave. My uncle doesn't need to know that we were even here," she pleaded.

He stopped and faced her once more. "Lillith, I am not a man who gives up easily."

"I can see that."

"I also want this alliance more than anything, but I was hoping to talk to Arthur and convince him to let us be married instead."

"Y-you were?" Suddenly she felt relief. "So, you're not going to cause trouble because he tricked you?"

"Nay. Not now, anyway. I need this alliance. And although I don't like being deceived, I will not confront him about it at this time."

"Thank you, Blaze."

"However, I want to be clear. If I can't convince him to change his mind, I will go through with the wedding with Serena after all. I need this alliance, Lillith. My future as a knight depends on it."

"Oh. I see," said Lillith, now feeling heartbroken. If things couldn't be changed, Lillith was going to live in misery the rest of her life. Seeing Serena married to Blaze instead of her was going to kill her.

"Lady Lillith?" Sir Gunderic opened the door to the keep. "What are you doing here? I thought you were at Skull Manor with your sister."

"We thought we'd stop by and make a quick visit," said Blaze.

Sir Gunderic's eyes opened wide. "Lord Payne?"

"Aye, it's me. The man to whom you are now aligned. I take it Lord Arthur is inside?"

"Well, yes, but . . ."

Blaze didn't wait to be introduced. He pushed past the knight and made his way to the great hall.

"Excuse me, Sir Gunderic," said Lillith, running past him,

leaving a trail of rain water in her wake. "Blaze, wait. Let's think things through before you say anything." Before she could stop him, he'd entered the great hall. Everyone became quiet, and her uncle stood up on the dais.

"Lord Payne?" asked Arthur. "What are you doing here?"

"It's the warlock," she heard one of the kitchen maids whisper. Everyone moved away from them.

"Lord Bonnel, I wanted to come in person to thank you for betrothing me to your niece. Even though, you failed to make it clear at the time which one of the girls I was marrying."

"Blaze, no," she whispered.

"Arthur? What's going on?" asked Lillith's mother, looking up in surprise.

"I don't believe I've summoned you, Payne," growled Arthur. "And you are dripping water all over my floor."

"Lillith? Did you two ride here in the rain?" Beatrice jumped up and ran over to greet them. Arthur reluctantly followed.

"Mother," said Lillith, giving her a slight hug, not wanting to get her wet.

"Where is Serena?" Beatrice looked around.

"She's back at the manor," Lillith answered. "I was out for a ride and it started to rain. Lord Blaze came to look for me. We came here to get out of the rain since it was closer than the manor. I hope you don't mind."

"Of course not, my dear." Her mother called a servant girl over. "Please make sure Lady Lillith gets a dry change of clothes. Then she will join us for the meal. Sir Gunderic will find something dry for you to wear, Lord Blaze."

"Never mind," said Blaze. "It's really only my cloak that is wet." He made a big show of removing it, purposely shaking water on the floor, probably just to rile Arthur. Lillith didn't want to leave her uncle and Blaze together. She might need to intervene if trouble started.

"I'm fine too, Mother. Really," she said. "Mayhap just a cup of mead would be nice."

"You'll sit up at the dais with us. Both of you," said Beatrice, putting her arm around Lillith and escorting her to the head table. She looked back to see Blaze following, and her uncle reluctantly doing the same.

"I thought we'd talk about the wedding while we're here," said Blaze as he seated himself right next to Arthur. Lillith thought she'd better sit next to him instead of with her mother.

"There's plenty of time for that, Payne," grumbled Arthur, sitting back down, taking a big swig of wine.

"I thought the sooner the better. I mean for the alliance and all. It's so nice that the feud is finally over." Blaze picked up a cup and held it out for the cupbearer to fill.

"Yes. Nice," said Lillith, looking out at everyone staring at them with scowls on their faces. It was clear that the rest of the inhabitants of Alderwood weren't so happy about this idea. It would take time for them to accept Blaze.

"You are all invited to join us for the wedding at Skull Manor." Blaze took a drink of wine, not even looking at Lillith. "However, since I've been tricked, I want to marry your niece, Lillith instead of Serena.

Her uncle was drinking and almost choked, spitting out his wine.

"Blaze, not here. Not now," Lillith whispered, knowing this conversation should be held in private.

"Lord Payne, what do you mean you were tricked?" asked Beatrice, obviously not knowing what Arthur had done.

"Your new lord, Lady Bonnel, decided to fool me, making me believe I was agreeing to marry Lillith instead of Serena."

"What? Arthur, is this true?" asked Beatrice.

"I might have forgot to mention which girl he'd marry in the proposal, but it was written as plain as day in the final contract," said Arthur, looking madder than hell. "You signed that contract, if I must remind you, Lord Payne."

"You purposely wrote in Serena's name at the last minute, knowing I wouldn't see it. I want you to change it to Lillith."

"Oh, my," gasped Beatrice. "Lord Payne, my daughter, Lillith is already betrothed to someone else."

"That's right, Payne," growled Arthur. "The contracts are binding and cannot be changed."

"For your sake, I'd try," said Blaze in a low voice, swirling his wine around in his goblet.

"If I break the betrothal with the baron, we'll be at odds. I can't do that," said Arthur. "I have my reputation to uphold."

"Well, when I tell everyone you deceived me, you won't have a reputation to uphold, so don't worry about it," Blaze snarled.

"Arthur, isn't there something you can do?" asked Beatrice.

"Aye, please try, Uncle," said Lillith, getting involved. "I don't want to marry the baron. I want to marry Blaze."

"I'll have to get back to you on that," said Arthur, taking a drink of wine. "I have a lot going on. Besides, the baron is overseas fighting for the king right now, so there is no way to even contact him." He picked up his spoon and scooped some pottage onto his plate.

"How convenient," said Blaze.

"Blaze, please." Lillith put her hand on his. She didn't want any trouble, and could see Blaze growing more frustrated by the minute.

"Lillith, I really wish that you and Lord Payne would get into some dry clothes before you catch your deaths of cold," said Beatrice.

"Nay. We're leaving." Blaze stood up and Lillith followed. "Lord Bonnel, this is no way to start an alliance. You have deceived me, and it is not acceptable."

"You signed the contract, Payne," growled Arthur. "Now, if you're leaving, do so before you get any more water on my floor."

"Come on, Lillith," said Blaze, turning and walking at a brisk pace through the great hall, leaving Lillith standing there not knowing what to do or say.

"Uncle, please," she begged. "Isn't there something you can do?"

"I suggest you leave now, Lillith," said her uncle, telling her that he would do nothing to help matters in this case.

"Oh, Lillith." Her mother hurried over and hugged her. "I wish things could be different, but there really isn't anything Arthur can do."

"Nay. I suppose not," she said, feeling heartbroken. "Good-bye, Mother."

"Let us know when the wedding will be," called out her uncle as Lillith left the great hall.

Ten

BLAZE RODE BACK toward Skull Manor with his arms and cloak wrapped around Lillith since she sat in front of him on the horse. The rain had let up and it was only drizzling now. The reins of the slow horse were tied to his, and it trailed behind them.

He supposed he hadn't really thought Arthur would do anything to help him. Still, he had to try.

"I'm sorry things didn't work out the way we would have liked them to," said Lillith.

"Me too," he said, his mouth right up to her ear since their bodies were pressed together.

"Don't give up hope, Blaze. There must be a way to make it happen."

"I'm surprised to hear you say that after you seemed to hate me when I first saw you again at the cemetery."

"I thought I did, but after being with you again, I realized I could never hate you, Blaze."

"Well, there isn't anything I can do to change things," said Blaze. "I signed the contract and it is binding."

"You were tricked."

"Yes. But I was so excited to think I was marrying you that I didn't even read it. It's all my fault."

"Even if you had read it, I was still already betrothed to the baron. Oh, Blaze, this is horrible. What are we going to do?"

"I suppose we bide our time and put off my wedding as long as possible. Mayhap I can talk to the baron when he returns."

"Do you think that will make a difference?"

"Nay. Not really. And I'm sad to say that if I can't convince him to let me marry you, then I will be going ahead and marrying your sister – something I don't really want to do."

"I see." Lillith didn't like that idea at all of Blaze saying he'd still go through with the wedding to Serena.

"Lilly, you know I need this alliance. I have been through hard times and if I want to be accepted back by the earl and knighted, I have to do this."

"I understand."

"It is the only way I can fix my family's reputation."

"Blaze, there are the standing stones," she said spotting them through the trees. "Can we stop here? I want to see them again."

Blaze didn't want to do it, but he also didn't want to deny Lilly's request. He never could say no to her. "Well, all right, but just for a minute. This rain might get worse and we need to keep riding."

He wasn't at all sure he should be taking Lillith right to the stone circle, but since she'd already seen it, he supposed it didn't matter. He only hoped the pageboy would keep his mouth shut about what he saw.

He dismounted, and helped Lillith from the horse. It felt odd being here. Blaze had not participated in the Samhain ceremony since his mother left five years ago. After his mother had been accused of cursing Lillith's brother, Blaze ignored the ring of stones entirely. Now, his mother had returned into his life, and she would expect him to participate in the Samhain traditions with the rest of the coven once again.

"I want to see it, closer." Lillith walked right past him, heading for the center of the circle.

"Lilly, nay. Wait," he told her. "You can't just parade right into the center of the circle."

"Why not?" she asked with a shrug. "It's so intriguing that I want to walk inside it."

"This is kind of a sacred spot. But I suppose if you respect it, it will be fine."

"Sacred for witches," she said.

"I really don't like that word."

"What else would you call your people?"

"I am no different from anyone else, and grew up more like my father than my mother. I wouldn't call my mother a witch either. That has such a negative connotation."

"Then what would you call her?"

"She is more of a . . . nature healer. She knows how to use plants and herbs and gives thanks to all living things. You see, some people are more in tune with the earth than others."

"That's odd to hear you talk that way. Are you sure you're not more like your mother than you think?"

"I don't condone everything my mother does, believe me."

"Like her card readings?"

"Aye. But I swear she does no harm and never makes anything bad happen even though it seems no one believes her."

"Well, what is this circle used for?" She ambled inside and Blaze followed.

"It is used for ceremonies at certain times of the year. One being Beltane, which happens in May, between spring and summer. Another important one is Samhain, that happens after the harvest and before the dead of winter, which is now."

"Like All Hallows' Day," said Lillith.

"Yes. Sort of. That is the Christian's version. Samhain is an ancient Celtic tradition. It's a time to prepare for winter, when the summer has ended. Crops are harvested and the livestock is brought down from the hills for slaughtering or breeding."

"And sacrificing? With a bonfire?" she asked.

"I know what you're thinking, Lilly. It is just a way of giving thanks to the land and ensuring a bountiful harvest next year. In ancient times the bonfire was even called bone fire, you know."

"But sacrificing?" She looked up to him with wide, innocent eyes, and blinked twice in succession, waiting for his answer.

"You eat meat, don't you?"

"Yes. Of course."

"We are talking about the livestock here. Pigs and sheep, not people."

A loud crash of thunder made them both jump. It even scared the horses. Unfortunately, they hadn't secured the reins to a tree, and the horses took off through the woods without them.

"Nay!" cried Lillith, starting to go after them, but Blaze grabbed her arm to stop her. "What are you doing, Blaze? We need to go find them."

"We will. Later. My horse will most likely go back to the manor. Yours will go too since they are hitched together. Right now, the sky is about to open up, and I suggest we take cover fast."

"Take cover? Where?" she asked, just as the rain came pouring down.

"This way," he told her, taking her by the hand and running toward a hill. They didn't stop until they were inside a small cave, and out of the pouring rain.

"We will stay dry here," said Blaze, looking out of the cave into the downpour. "Hopefully, it won't take too long for the storm to pass." He stared up at the sky.

"I'm not in a hurry." She walked over and looped her arm through his. "It gives me more time to spend with you."

He looked over to her and shook his head. "Lilly, you know I cherish every moment we are together. But it will not last. And we can't change things that are already in motion, though I tried my best to do so." He sat down on the floor of the cave and she sat down next to him, staring out at the rain, waiting for it to end.

"I know you're right. Thank you for trying, Blaze."

"I haven't given up yet," he said softly, playing with a twig he found on the cave floor.

They sat in silence for a few minutes, just watching the rain fall outside the cave entrance. It reminded Blaze of the times in the past when they'd been on an outing and gotten caught in a storm before they returned. He chuckled.

"What's so funny?" she asked.

"Do you remember that time we were caught in the rain and were so drenched we looked like drowned rats?"

She giggled. "Yes. And when we tried to sneak in to Alderwood Castle using the postern door, my gown got caught and ripped all the way up to my waist?"

They both laughed now. "I had a lot of explaining to do to your father, didn't I?"

"If it wasn't for me begging my mother to help us, I swear my father would have hanged you from the battlements."

Blaze boldly reached out and put his arm around Lillith's shoulders. She, in turn, leaned in to him, resting her head against his chest.

"Blaze?"

"Hmm?" He nuzzled his face against her hair, not caring that it was wet.

"I don't believe for a moment that your mother cursed my brother, Robert."

"Really." He looked at her from the corners of his eyes. "But you did believe it, didn't you? That's why you feared me and my family for the last five years and didn't even come near me?"

"I suppose I let my father convince me, and I shouldn't have. He was very superstitious and liked to blame the bad happenings in life on others. I don't think he could cope with death or disappointment. That is why he drank so much."

"I've never known you to be someone who didn't make her own choices and have her own opinions, Lilly."

"He forbade me to go near you."

"Your actions have really disappointed me. I thought I knew you." He slipped his arm off of her and continued to play with the twig.

"You do know me, Blaze. I'm the same Lilly I always was."

"Are you?" He raised a brow. "The Lilly I knew wouldn't be caught dead being betrothed to anyone she didn't want to marry."

"That's not fair. You know a woman has no say as to whom her father betroths her to. Why should I be any different?"

"You're right, I suppose. But I can't help thinking that maybe you wanted that betrothal with the baron after all." When she remained quiet, he knew his assumption was right. "I suppose I can't blame you. After all, the baron has so much more to offer. I don't even have a title, a castle, or anything that you deserve. I feel bad for your sister." He chuckled, but not because he thought it was funny.

"All right, I admit, mayhap I did want to marry the baron at first," she said with a sigh, looking away. "But it was only because my father hated you and your family so much, and I feared you."

"You feared me? How could you? You know I'd never do anything to hurt you."

"I do know that. I am embarrassed to have ever doubted that now. Honestly, I only agreed to it because I didn't want to become a nun, being so old and still unmarried. You know, my father would have had no qualms in sending me to a convent."

They both laughed at that, breaking the tension between them.

He looked back out at the rain. "I never gave up on us, Lilly. Even through the hard times, I had faith that we'd once again, someday, be together."

"And we are. Right here, right now," she said, putting her hand on his knee, but it didn't make him smile.

"You know what I mean."

"Kiss me, Blaze. Please," she said in a sultry whisper. "It is all I've been able to think about since you kissed me in the woods."

He looked at her lips and wanted this more than anything. But he knew if he kissed her, he wouldn't be able to stop. He would end up making love with her, right here on the cave floor. Lust roared in his veins. His heart about beat out of his chest.

He'd been dreaming of making love with Lilly for so long now. But now that he had the chance to do it, he couldn't.

"I can't," he said, quickly standing up before he was tempted to do something he would regret. "You are betrothed to another man, and I have no right to take what has been offered to him. The rain seems to be letting up now. I think we should go."

"Oh. All right," she said sounding very disappointed as Blaze helped her to her feet.

The sound of a bird's cry pierced the air, catching Blaze's attention. "That sounds like Ebony. I'll bet she found the horses nearby and is trying to tell me."

"Then we'd better hurry," said Lillith, following him out of the cave. Blaze didn't want to look at Lillith. He couldn't. It hurt too bad to turn her away. The way he just had. But what felt even worse was to know that what he really wanted, he could never have.

Eleven

"SISTER, WHERE HAVE YOU BEEN?" Serena ran up to meet Lillith, with Posy on her heels. "It's been hours since Milo returned. He said you were right behind him."

"Yes, what took so long?" asked Posy. "We were so worried about you. We knew you were with . . . " Posy stopped in midsentence, looking over Lillith's head to Blaze who was right behind her.

"Everything is fine," Lillith told them. "We were caught in the rain and stopped at Alderwood Castle to see Mother and Uncle Arthur." Lillith dismounted before Blaze had a chance to help her.

"You went home? With Blaze?" asked Serena, her jaw dropping.

"What did your uncle say?" asked Posy. "I'm sure he wasn't happy about it."

"That's nonsense, Posy," said Blaze. "Why should Arthur be anything but happy about seeing me?" He slid off the horse. "After all, I am betrothed to you now, Serena, so I am part of the family."

Lillith looked over at her sister, seeing her face pale. Serena reached out and grabbed on to Posy's arm.

The rain had stopped and the sun broke through the clouds.

"Lord Payne. Can I take your horse for you?" asked Orvyn, rushing over to meet them. Lillith noticed the stablemaster, having seen him on foot, slipping through the gate just before them. He had been coming from somewhere, and she wondered where he'd been. He was a pesky man who always seemed to be around without really being seen.

"Mother, there you are," said Blaze, making Lillith turn to look. Minerva was standing right there, and Lillith hadn't even seen her walk up. The woman wore a long gown that was wispy and flowed in the breeze. It was made from a dark purple cloth with patches of white lace embroidered on to it in the shape of moons and stars. While it was odd in nature, and not the normal type of clothing a lady would wear, Lillith rather liked it. Minerva cradled her black cat in her arms, petting its head.

"Your gown is pretty," Lillith told her. "I love purple."

"I remember," said Minerva. "Blaze's bedcurtains are still remembering it."

"Where did you get the gown?" asked Lillith.

"I make all my own clothes," said Minerva proudly. "I could make a gown like this for you too, my dear."

"Mother, that's not necessary," said Blaze in a warning voice, but the woman just continued.

"Why don't you join me in the solar later, and I will take your measurements and get started. Actually, I have an extra gown just like this that I don't know what to do with. I can alter it so it fits you."

"Well . . . I. . . ." Lillith looked over to her sister and Posy. They were both shaking their heads, warning her not to accept the offer. Blaze turned and walked away with his raven flying above him. "I do believe I'd like that, Lady Minerva," Lillith answered, wanting to get to know Blaze's mother better. Lillith remembered her from the time she spent here with Blaze when she was growing up, but Minerva always seemed preoccupied or distant and hadn't spoken much with Lillith. Mayhap this would be a good chance to do so now.

"Wonderful. I'll be off then." Minerva picked up her skirt and headed away, mumbling to herself. "There is so much to do. We need to start planning for the holiday festivities."

"What did she say?" asked Serena. "Was she talking about All Hallows' Day?"

"Aye. I believe so," Lillith answered, knowing Minerva really meant Samhain, but Lillith didn't want to mention it to her sister and handmaid.

Minerva stopped in her tracks and turned around. "Lady Serena, I'd like to get to know you better since you will be marrying my son soon. I look forward to your help in planning the festivities." Her cat started meowing, so Lillith reached out to pet it.

"This is Sam. Short for Samhain," she said with a smirk and headed away.

"Lillith!" squeaked Serena in a half-whisper. "She just said Samhain. That proves she's a witch."

"Plus, she has a black cat. It's probably her familiar," added Posy.

"Sister, I don't want to help her plan any kind of festivities. You've got to get me out of here. Please." Horror filled Serena's eyes.

"You aren't going anywhere," said Lillith. "This will be your home now, and we have a lot of work to do before the wedding."

"Nay! I'm done with this ridiculous plan. I want to go home." She turned to head to the stable, but Lillith grabbed her arm and squeezed it tightly, talking to her sister in a low voice. "This wedding will give Blaze the chance to have a life he's longed for. Without it, the feud will never end."

"You're hurting me, Lillith. Let go."

"Not before you promise not to cause trouble."

"You want me to marry Blaze?" asked Serena in confusion. "I thought you were still in love with him."

"If I can't marry him, then you will. Now, push your obstinance aside and get to know him and his family."

"Lady Lillith, you are asking too much from her," protested Posy.

"Nay, I'm not. I am asking her to do what I would if I were lucky enough to be in her position."

"You wouldn't be asking me anything if you knew what we know," spat Serena.

"What does that mean?" Lillith released her hold on her sister's arm.

"Go on and tell her, Posy," said Serena, straightening her hair and trying to pull a wrinkle out of her gown.

"Tell me what?" asked Lillith.

"We will tell you, but not here." Posy looked around, scanning the area. "Come back to our chamber, quickly. Follow us and we'll show you what we found."

"Yes," said Serena. "You're not going to believe it."

"Won't believe what?"

"Shhhh, just follow us, sister." Serena took Lillith's arm and all but dragged her into the manor and up to their bedchamber. It wasn't until Posy had closed and locked the door that they told her what all this secrecy was about.

"Will you two tell me why you're acting so odd?" asked Lillith, plopping down on the bed. She picked up a leather bag with a shoulder strap that was hers and started to dig through it, looking for a brush.

"While you were out, Posy and I had a chance to look for evidence," explained Serena.

"Evidence?" asked Lillith. "Explain."

"Evidence that Blaze was involved in the death of our father, and that he is a witch. Posy, show her what we found."

"Aye, my lady." Posy hurried over to a trunk and opened it, bringing out something wrapped in a soft piece of cloth.

"What is it?" asked Lillith curiously.

"Just look at this." Posy pulled a black beeswax candle out and held it up for her to see.

"It's a candle. So?" asked Lillith, finding her brush and running it through her windblown hair.

"It's black," spat Posy. "Have you ever seen a black candle before?"

"No. Not really," she answered.

"It's used by witches when they summon spirits," said Posy.

"Stop it," said Lillith, waving her hand through the air. "You two are out of your mind."

"That's not all Posy found. Show her," Serena said to the handmaid.

Next, Posy pulled out Blaze's dagger with the moon and stars and skull carved into the hilt. Lillith felt like she was going to retch.

"Where did you get that?" gasped Lillith.

"It was in Lord Blaze's room," Serena relayed the information. "It's the dagger Milo saw with blood on it. It was on the ground next to father."

"Milo identified it an hour ago," added Posy. "He also told us you found a stone circle in the woods."

Lillith could have groaned aloud. She had hoped Milo wouldn't tell anyone about that.

"You two had no right going into Blaze's solar and rummaging through his trunk," spat Lilly.

"I didn't do it. It was Posy," said Serena. "And how did you know she found it in his trunk?"

"That's right," said Posy. "We didn't tell you exactly where we found it."

"Oh. I – I just supposed that's where it would be."

"Lillith!" Serena held her hand over her mouth. Then, she slowly lowered it. "You knew this dagger was there, didn't you? You must have found it in Lord Blaze's room when you went there earlier, and you didn't even mention it to us."

"Did you?" asked Posy, putting her hands on her hips.

"I did not find it," she said, then let out a deep breath. "But I won't lie. I knew it was there."

"How could you?" asked Serena. "I don't understand."

"Blaze caught me in his solar and knew what I was doing there. He presented the dagger to me."

"Oh, my!" gasped Serena. "So he admitted he is guilty."

"Nay, just the opposite," said Lillith. "He is not guilty of anything." She explained the situation to them.

"Nay," said Posy. "He told you this wild story, and you believe it?"

"I do," said Lillith standing up for what she believed, just like Blaze pointed out that she always used to do. It was time for her to be that girl again. "I know Blaze is a good man. He told me he didn't do it, and also that he would never harm me or anyone in my family." She took the blade from Posy and wrapped it back up and stuck it into her leather bag. "Now, I will take care of this. And I don't want to hear another bad word about Blaze or his family. They will be our family, too. and the two of you need to learn to accept it."

There was a knock at the door and all three of them jumped and just looked at each other but didn't say a word.

"Lady Lillith, I'm ready for you now to start alterations on your gown," came Minerva's muffled voice from the corridor. "Also, Blaze would like Serena to accompany him for a walk through the orchard."

"Nay," whispered Serena, her blue eyes growing wide in fear. "I don't want to go."

"You have to, Serena. You're his betrothed now. It is your duty."

"But I can't go unescorted."

"Posy will go with you." Lillith closed up her bag with the dagger inside it. "We'll be right there," she called out.

"Lady Lillith, I wish you'd listen to us," whispered Posy. "We are not safe here."

"On the contrary, I believe we are safer here than anywhere," said Lillith. "Now, let's go," she said, hustling them to the door. "And everyone, try to be friendly."

Lillith opened the door to find Minerva with her black cat in her arms once again. The cat hissed and jumped down, running through the corridor.

"I wonder what's spooked Sam," said Minerva. "He's usually not so skittish. I suppose it's just because he's feeling the thinning of the veil this time of year."

Lillith noticed Serena staring with her mouth opened wide.

"Have a nice walk in the orchard." Lillith turned the girl around and gave her a gentle push in the opposite direction. Serena and Posy hurried away.

"Well, shall we go to the ladies solar?" asked Lillith with a smile.

"We're not going there. I've already got everything set up in Blaze's solar," Minerva told her.

"Right," she said, closing the door to the chamber. The last place she wanted to be was there. After Blaze turned down her kiss, she felt embarrassed by her actions. Being in the man's bedchamber was only going to make matters worse.

"There's no time to waste. We have much to do. Now come along, Lady Lillith," said Minerva, taking her by the arm and pulling her out of the room. "And as soon as this gown is finished, there are wedding plans to make."

"Oh, I think Blaze said the wedding wouldn't be for a while yet."

"Well, then we'll work on the preparations for Samhain. I mean, All Hallows' Day."

"Of course," mumbled Lillith as they walked, thinking she would like to know more about Samhain, and Minerva might be the exact person to ask about it.

Twelve

BLAZE STROLLED through the orchard with Serena on his arm and the handmaid following close behind. He was only doing this to try to get to know the girl since it looked like he'd be marrying her instead of Lillith. She had always been so shy, that she'd never even talked to him when they were children. Lillith had been talkative, laughed a lot, and was always wanting to go on an adventure. Serena, on the other hand, had kept to herself. Most of the time she was in her bedchamber napping, he'd been told.

"So what do you think of my orchards?" asked Blaze, stopping under an apple tree. Serena held on to his arm, but he could tell she really didn't want to do it. Blaze's servants worked picking apples, watching them curiously.

"Very nice," said Serena, letting go of his arm and pretending to fix her hair. "Don't you think so, Posy?" He noticed that she tried her best to pull in the handmaid in for support.

"Hrumph," mumbled Posy, not looking at all happy to be here. "The sun isn't good for my lady's skin. I'll need to take her back to the manor to get her a proper head covering."

"Of course. By all means, don't let me stop you," said Blaze, not feeling comfortable with this at all. Plus, he could see how much they feared him and it was ridiculous. "After all, I'll want my bride in prime condition on our wedding night," he said, just to goad them. He saw the terror in Serena's eyes as the girl grabbed onto her handmaid, and they hurried away, almost bumping into Lillith and his mother.

"Serena, where are you going?" Lillith called after them.

"I've got to get in out of the sun," said Serena, not bothering to slow down or to turn around.

"But it's not even that sunny," said Lillith with a shrug.

Blaze walked over to join them.

"I think I frightened your sister," he said with a chuckle.

"Blaze, what did you do?" asked Minerva.

"I'm tired of them fearing me for no reason at all. I just thought I'd give them more to talk about, that's all. Now, tell me what you two have been up to." He reached up and pulled an apple off the tree, rubbing it on his sleeve to clean it.

"Your mother is altering one of her gowns for me to wear on All Hallows' Eve," said Lillith, sounding excited.

"Really." He handed the apple to Lillith and reached up and took another off the tree. "Mother, what else is going on? I hope you're not giving Lillith a hard time." He rubbed the second apple on his tunic now.

"Nay, she's not," Lillith answered before Minerva could answer. "We are actually planning festivities for All Hallows' Eve. I am helping her."

"I'm not sure that is a good idea." Blaze scowled. "We don't really celebrate the holiday at Skull Manor. Not anymore."

"Why not?" asked Lillith taking a bite out of the apple.

"Yes, why not, Blaze?" Minerva took the apple he handed her. "After all, we always used to do so when I lived at the manor. By the way, I've noticed that you've really let things slide around here. The entire manor needs a good cleaning."

"I can help with that," said Lillith, wanting to lend a hand.

"Nay," growled Blaze. "I have servants for that. You are a lady and shouldn't be doing such work."

"Blaze, we have only one more day to prepare for Samhain – I mean All Hallows' Eve. I'd like you to help us."

"Mother," he said, his eyes flashing over to Lillith.

"It's all right, Blaze," said Lillith. "I know about Samhain. Or at least a little."

"She's been asking me about it," said Minerva.

God's eyes, he couldn't believe this. "What did you say?"

"I didn't say much," answered Minerva. "I figured you'd get angry with me if I said too much, so you'll have to answer her questions, Blaze."

There was silence between them, and thankfully Lillith changed the subject.

"Won't you help us with the preparations for All Hallows' Eve, Blaze?" Lillith smiled at him and gave him that irresistible little pout that could get him to do anything at all.

"Aye. Of course, I'll help," he said in defeat.

"Lady Lillith, did you know that if you peel an apple this time of year and throw the peels over your shoulder, you'll see the initial of the man you'll marry?" asked Minerva.

"Nay, I don't think that really works," said Lillith.

"That's nonsense," spat Blaze.

"And another way to see your future husband, is to take a bite of apple and then look into something that makes a reflection while standing at a fire on All Hallows' Eve," continued Minerva. "You'll see him clear as day in the reflection."

"Stop it, Mother." Blaze didn't like the way this conversation was going.

"Serena and I used to throw hazelnuts into the fire on All Hallows' Eve," explained Lillith.

"Whatever for?" asked Blaze.

"If they pop, the man you've asked about loves you. If they burn, he does not."

"That is nothing but child's play," said Blaze. "I'm going to take a walk up the hill to check on the livestock. Now that it's the end of the season, we'll have to bring the sheep out of the summer pasture soon."

"I'll talk to the servants and have them gather up all the turnips in the field so we can start carving them for Samhain," said Minerva, looking around the orchard.

"You mean All Hallows' Eve," grumbled Blaze.

"Yes, of course." Minerva smiled.

"I'll help you," said Lillith.

"Nay, it's a beautiful day, my dear. Why don't you keep Blaze company instead? I will ask your sister to work with me." Minerva didn't wait for an answer. Instead, she turned and hurried away.

"I think my mother's lack of subtility is one of her biggest flaws," said Blaze.

"Don't you want me to accompany you?" asked Lillith, her smile fading. "I suppose I can go back to the manor. Although, I wouldn't mind taking a walk in nature with you. Unless you don't want me along."

Blaze could think of nothing he'd like more. Every minute he spent with Lillith was time he would cherish forever. "Of course. I'd be grateful for the company." He held out his arm and Lillith took it, much easier in acceptance than her sister had. They strolled up the hill to the pasture where the sheep were grazing.

While Skull Manor wasn't as big as a castle, it was still a good size. Most of the neighboring villagers answered to Alderwood Castle. But there was still a small village for the serfs with cottages of wattle and daub that housed those who served Blaze's family.

They walked past his servants and up the hill, getting stares since he wasn't with his betrothed. Blaze no longer cared. The woman he wanted to be with was on his arm, even if she could never be his wife. He would spend as much time with her as he could now, before her betrothed returned to England.

"It is just as beautiful up here on the hilltop as I remember it from when we were children." Lillith's eyes lit up as they reached the crest of the hill, looking down at his manor and fields of crops below.

"Do you remember we used to come up here to hide when you didn't want to go home?" he asked with a chuckle. "My parents used to spend hours searching through the manor looking for us."

"I do," said Lillith, plopping down on the ground and lying back, looking up at the clouds. "We used to see objects in the clouds, too. Come on, Blaze, join me. Let's try it now."

"Lillith, we're no longer children," he objected. "That is not something adults do."

"Well, it should be. After all, just because we're adults doesn't mean we can't use our imaginations and have fun. Come on." She patted the ground next to her.

Blaze looked around, seeing nothing but livestock. He probably shouldn't do this, but who would really know? "All right. But just for a moment," he said, lying down next to her and looking up at the sky. It was a beautiful day with puffy white clouds laden across a bright, blue sky. The crisp autumn breeze felt fresh and invigorating.

"What do you see?" asked Lillith. "Oh, look!" She pointed upward. "It's a big dragon. Do you see it?"

"Aye," he answered, seeing something else as well. "And there is a rabbit riding a dog."

"A what?" she asked with a giggle. "Where? I don't see it."

"Right there."

"Nay."

"This way," he said, leaning up on one elbow and gently taking her chin in his hand. He turned her face in the right direction. "Do you see it now?"

"Aye," she said with a laugh. "It really is a bunny riding a hound." When she turned her eyes back to him, their faces were close together. Blaze found himself lost in the clear depths of her bright blue eyes. Memories flooded his mind of all the time he'd spent with Lillith. Soon, it would be all he had to remember her by. Once she was married, he'd never be able to spend time with her again. They'd made plans long ago. They had dreams at one time. But all that was gone now, and naught but childhood fun that would fade with each day that passed.

"Blaze," she said, staring at his mouth. "This seems like old times again. It feels so right to be with you. Like nothing has changed."

"I know," he said, now looking at her mouth too. He could no longer stop himself from kissing her. He moved his face closer to hers and saw her eyes flickering shut. Then he touched her lips with his, and when he did, all his troubles seemed to disappear. A feeling of completeness flowed through him. This was his Lillith, and he never wanted to let her go.

Rolling on to his side, his long hair hung down around them as he kissed her again – this time deeper. He boldly let his tongue enter her mouth. She accepted him instead of pushing him away.

"Oh, Lillith, you have no idea how much I've missed you."

"I've missed you, too, Blaze."

He tucked her hair behind her ear and stroked her soft cheek, looking deeply into her eyes. He was sure he could see all the way to the depths of her soul.

"All I've dreamed of since the feud started, was for it to end so I could have you in my arms and be kissing you, just like this," he told her.

"Me too," she said softly, reaching up and kissing him passionately. Her desire for him showed. It seemed just as strong as his desire for her. His hand slid down her cheek, grazing past her neck and settling atop one breast. She seemed to like it and didn't stop him. Her breathing became deeper. Then he placed gentle kisses down her neck, flicking his tongue out to touch the top of her collarbone as he filled his hand with her mound and gave it a light squeeze.

"Oooooh," she moaned, arching her back, pushing her breast deeper into his embrace. He felt himself stir and harden beneath his belt. He wanted Lillith badly.

"Lillith, I want you."

"I want you, too," she answered in a breathy whisper. He was lost in the moment and probably would have taken the foreplay further if he hadn't heard what she had to say next. "I want you, not Baron Bancroft."

Lillith felt Blaze's body still, and then he quickly moved his hand off her breast and abruptly sat up.

"Blaze? Is something wrong?" She sat up, seeing him shaking his head and running a hand through his long hair.

"We can't do this, Lilly Bee," he said, using the name for her that always made her heart swell. "It's no longer right. We are both promised to someone else now. We can't be together. Not anymore. It's too late." He got to his feet.

"Of course, we can. We belong together. I feel it and I know you do, too."

"Those feelings don't matter. We are both betrothed to other people, in case you are forgetting." His dark eyes stared down at her in disappointment.

Lillith felt her heart sink in her chest. She hadn't forgotten. Then again, neither had she done anything to stop what just happened between them either. Did that make her a bad person? And did she really care?

"Blaze, we have always been honest with each other in the past, haven't we?"

"Yes. Of course we have."

"Well, I need to be honest with you now. I don't want Serena to marry you. I am jealous of the betrothal, and part of me is very wicked, feeling like I want to ruin it and stop the wedding from happening."

"That doesn't make you a bad person, Lilly. However, you should be happy for your sister."

"I know. I am ashamed of myself for even kissing you when she's to be your bride soon."

"I didn't stop you. I'm no better."

"This is too hard, Blaze. I am not sure if I'll be able to accept you two together. It hurts too much."

He reached out and stroked her cheek once more. "I told you I would never hurt you, Lilly, and I won't."

"I know that. But why are you saying this?"

"What I'm trying to tell you is that I will break the alliance. I won't marry your sister."

"Nay! If you do that, you'll never get the earl to accept you as a knight. Plus, the feud will only continue."

"I would rather live in hell then to know I did anything to hurt you. I'll send a missive to your uncle anon. You and your sister should pack your bags, because I'm sorry, but I am sending you both home."

He left her standing there, heading down the hill to the manor. Lillith felt like she wanted to cry. This isn't what she wanted. She hadn't meant for him to give up everything he longed for at her expense.

She had to do something to stop him. Lillith wouldn't let Blaze go through with this, because it would only ruin his life. That is the last thing she wanted to see. Hurrying down the hill after him, she knew only one person who could stop Blaze from taking such drastic measures. She needed to find Minerva, and she had to do it before it was too late.

Thirteen

"LADY MINERVA?" Lillith knocked gently on the door to Blaze's solar, knowing the woman was there working on her gown. Orvyn had told her Minerva already returned from the field where the servants brought back a wagon load of turnips for the festival.

The door opened, and with it came a whoosh of air in Lillith's face, filled with the scent of incense.

"Lillith. I was expecting you. Come in, please."

"Y-you were?" Lillith looked around the room. Candles burned on every table. A trail of smoke rose up from a small dish where what looked like dry leaves were smoldering.

"Yes," said Minerva. "Your gown is ready to try on. Come in."

"Oh," she said, thinking the woman knew why she was really there. "Oh, it's beautiful," she said, when Minerva held up the purple gown. It looked just like the one she wore, but Minerva had altered it to fit her and added a big lavender, satin bow on the back. It had patches and lace decorating the velvet that was in the shape of moons and stars. "How on earth did you finish it so quickly?"

"I didn't need to do much at all. Do you like it?" she asked.

"I do."

"Put it on."

"Well, all right." While Minerva helped Lillith dress, Lillith relayed the true reason of why she was there.

"So, you're saying my son is going to call off the betrothal to your sister?" Minerva took a step back and narrowed her eyes. "Why would he do that?"

"I think it was my fault," she admitted. "I told him I was jealous that Serena was marrying him. I also said I didn't think I could accept them being together and that it would hurt too much."

"And Blaze is still in love with you and doesn't want to hurt you."

"Yes. We kissed," she told Minerva, picking up a crystal sitting on the table to inspect it. There were many gemstones in a circle, some of them in various colors.

"I see. Well, we have a problem here, don't we?"

"I agree. I don't want Blaze to break the betrothal, honest, I don't."

"Yet you don't want him to marry your sister either."

She shook her head and placed the crystal back down on the table. The cat watched her from its perch atop the bed. "Why do you have all these stones? They are so pretty."

"Each one holds a different vibration," said Minerva. "Did you know just by holding them, they can help heal things that might be ailing you?"

"Really?" She wasn't sure if she should believe this or not because it sounded so far-fetched.

"Here, my dear, this one is for you." Minerva held up a chain with a crystal pendant dangling from the end. It will help to keep good energy around you. Hold it when something is troubling you. It will help calm you and bring goodness into your life."

"Oh, no, I couldn't. But it is beautiful."

Minerva lowered the chain. "You're not afraid of it, are you? These stones help to balance emotions and keep one in a state of happiness as well."

"Well, all right. Why not?" she said, needing this in her life right now. Minerva clasped the chain around her neck. Lillith's hand went right to the crystal pendant, fingering it. "It seems like it's getting warmer."

"It is absorbing your energy. It is also a form of protection."

Lillith wasn't sure if this was something she should be wearing, but she rather liked it. It went well with the dress. Therefore, she accepted it without any more objections.

"Thank you, Lady Minerva. I appreciate all you are doing for me."

"I realized I wasn't as friendly toward you in the past as I could have been. Mayhap I can make it up to you now. After all, you'll be family."

"Not me. Not really. But my sister will be." She fingered the crystal pendant, hoping all her worries were being whisked away. Then, she realized how silly she was being. Nothing she could do would change the circumstances. Lillith dropped the crystal and it thunked against her chest.

"You realize that if Blaze breaks the betrothal, word will get out that he doesn't honor his agreements," said Minerva. "And once the earl hears this, my son will never be considered for knighthood. All Blaze has ever wanted was to follow in his father's footsteps."

"I know," said Lillith, feeling really bad now about the way she'd reacted. "The feud will also continue, and I want nothing more than for it to end."

"If it continues, I'll be sent away again." Minerva snapped closed the lid of her sewing box. "We need to change Blaze's mind quickly. Help me blow out these candles. We have to find him and stop him from making a big mistake."

* * *

"Put those boxes of turnips over here," instructed Blaze, pointing to one of the trestle tables in the great hall. The servants all gathered around with their children near the table. Blaze had warriors and servants living at the manor, but no knights or nobles. Most of them had all left after the feud started or when his father died. Therefore, Blaze catered to the servants and their families, and also the villagers, wanting them to have what they normally wouldn't be allowed to have or do.

"Children, gather around," said Minerva, swooping into the room, commanding attention the way she always did. "We're going to hollow out the turnips and carve faces into them."

Blaze turned to look at her and saw Lillith right behind her. They were both wearing gowns that matched. The only difference was the big bow on Lillith's curvy backside. He groaned. While Lillith looked beautiful dressed this way, Blaze wasn't sure he liked the fact she looked like his mother. Or a witch.

"Oh, I want to carve a turnip too," said Serena from the other side of the table. "But I want to make a handsome face in it, not a scary one."

"Go ahead," said Blaze, glad the girl was actually smiling instead of looking scared to death of him.

"These are some of the biggest turnips I've ever seen." Serena picked one up to inspect it. "Posy, help me choose. I want the best one."

"Aye, my lady," said the handmaid, trying to swish Minerva's fat black cat away as it hopped up to the table and started slinking around, rubbing up against the vegetables.

"Why do we do carve turnips?" asked a little girl, tugging on Blaze's tunic, looking up to him with wide eyes.

Blaze's eyes shot over to his mother. He wasn't sure he wanted to explain this.

"Go ahead, son. Tell her the tradition," said Minerva. "She's too young to even know about it."

"Well," said Blaze, clearing his throat. "After the turnips are hollowed out, scary faces are carved into them. On All Hallows' Eve, candles are put inside the turnips and lit. Then they are placed on windowsills and doorsteps."

"Why?" asked the little girl, not letting up with her questions.

"It's to . . . it's to . . ."

"It's to ward away the evil spirits that might come through the thinning veil from the land of the dead," came a sweet voice from behind him.

Blaze turned to see Lillith standing there with a smile spread across her face.

"Lilly," said Blaze in a mere whisper. "You look . . . nice." She looked beautiful as always and he didn't have the heart to say she looked like a witch.

"I'm here to help in planning and carrying out the festivities," said Lillith. "After all, All Hallows' Eve is tomorrow and we have so much to do to get ready."

Blaze frowned. "You won't be here so what does it matter? I told you, I'm sending you and your sister back home. I think you should both get packing right now. I'll send for my scribe to write the missive, breaking off the betrothal."

"Blaze, you are not breaking this alliance!" scolded his mother as the crowd busied themselves choosing turnips to carve. Her hands went to her waist.

"This is none of your business, Mother. Now, stay out of it."

"It is my business because it will affect everyone and everything, not just you. Don't you see if you call off the wedding, it is going to cause a lot of trouble?"

He looked over to Lillith, thinking about what had transpired up on the hill. All he could think about was how upset and sad she was by this betrothal. He didn't want her to be sad. She deserved happiness in life more than anyone.

"I'm sorry," said Blaze. "I just can't go through with it. No matter what the consequences."

"Then for heaven's sake, at least wait until after Samhain," spat Minerva.

"Mother!"

"All Hallows' Eve," she corrected herself. "The cooks have been busy all day baking soul cakes, and the children are so excited to be celebrating again. You have let the manor fall into disrepair, and you haven't seen to the needs of your people for the last five years. You are not acting at all like a lord."

"In case you're forgetting, I just inherited the title," Blaze reminded her. "If things aren't the way you like them, don't blame me. Father was the one who let things go, ever since you left. Whether you believe it or not, your leaving here affected him so much that he was never the same after that day."

"Really. Well, nice to know that," she said, being as cool as she always was and showing little emotion. Lillith had said Blaze didn't show emotion. Mayhap that was one thing he'd inherited from his mother after all. "Don't ruin the holiday for everyone else with your decision, Blaze."

"Please. Listen to your mother," begged Lillith. "A few more days isn't going to make a difference. Let's try to forget about all our troubles and for the next few days just enjoy the time we have together. All of us."

Blaze took in his surroundings. Everyone hurried around the great hall with smiles on their faces. Children giggled and chased each other while one of the musicians played the hurdygurdy, filling the room with cheery music. His cooks brought large trays of freshly baked soul cakes from the kitchen and placed them atop a table, shooing the children away from them while the cakes cooled.

The women chatted while they decorated the great hall with garland strung from acorns, seeds, and dried flowers. The men worked together hauling in dried stalks of barley and wheat that they bundled and placed in every corner of the room. Blaze's raven had flown in through an open window and sat atop a beam, inspecting everything going on below her.

Everyone seemed so happy and was working together. This is the way it was supposed to be. He hadn't seen anything like this in a long time now.

"My lord, the men want to know if they can start building the bonfire in the courtyard for tomorrow's festivities," asked Emery, walking up with Barnaby.

"The alewives will be bringing spiced wine and cider from town later today as well," said Barnaby.

"Oh, I hope they added lots of cinnamon and nutmeg," said Lillith, looking so excited. "It gives it such a good flavor."

"Yes, make sure they add the spices tonight so it has time to be absorbed into the liquid before it is used," agreed Minerva.

"My lord?" asked Emery again.

Blaze felt like he was in a dream. Lillith looked like lady of the manor, and she was getting along so well with his mother. Everyone was happy. There was no quarreling or anyone whispering bad things behind his back.

"Yes. Yes, go ahead," he told his men, swiping his hand through the air.

Lillith walked up and laid her hand on his arm. "Does this mean you'll let us stay for the celebration?" she asked.

"I guess so. But only for a few days. Then, you'll leave as planned."

"Thank you, Blaze." Lillith stood on her tiptoes and gave him a kiss on the cheek.

"Do you really think you should have done that, Lilly?" he asked in a low voice. His eyes scanned the room.

"No one saw it. Besides, I'm sure no one really cares," she said, with a wink.

A little girl tugged on Lillith's skirt. "Will you help me pick out a turnip to carve?"

"Well, I suppose so." Lillith looked up to Blaze as if she were silently asking permission.

"Go ahead," said Blaze, holding out his arm. "I don't want to stop anyone from enjoying themselves."

"Will you join us?" asked Lillith with hope in her voice.

"Yes, Blaze, carve a turnip. You used to love doing this as a child," said Minerva.

"I remember," said Lillith, her eyes lighting up. "One year,

Blaze carved a heart in a turnip and gave it to me. When it was lit from inside, a beautiful heart shape lit up the ground."

"I'll join you," said Blaze, longing to spend more time with Lillith. "But I was a child then. I'm not carving hearts into a turnip now."

"What will you carve?" asked the little girl.

Blaze reached out and swooped up the child, making her giggle as he held her in his arms. "Well, now, you'll just have to wait and see, won't you?"

When he looked back at Lillith, he swore he saw her wiping a tear from her eye.

Fourteen

LILLITH ENJOYED BEING INCLUDED in the decorating of the manor for All Hallows' Eve. After helping the children carve out turnips, she made sure the servants had apples and a trough brought to the stable for the apple bobbing, which was one of her favorite things to do. She was good at it, and wanted to show off in front of Blaze.

She went with Blaze to the kitchen now at his request.

"Why are we going here?" she asked.

"I want to make certain my cooks are making enough soul cakes for the celebration," he told her. "There are many poor, as well as beggars that will come by the manor on All Hallows' Eve."

"If you haven't been celebrating for the past five years, I'm surprise they still come by at all."

"Word gets out. They'll be here," he assured her.

Children and the poor would come begging for the sweet soul cakes, offering a prayer for dead loved ones in return.

"Let's see how they taste." Blaze took a hand-sized bun off the cooling table. It had a cross made from currants on top. He took a bite and then held the soul cake up to her mouth. Her hands closed over his as she brought her mouth closer.

"Careful. It's still hot," he warned her.

His scent of leather and fresh air filled her senses, making her heady. His small action of sharing food with her made her feel as if she were his lady, even though she knew that would never be true.

"Yes. It's still hot," she said, blowing on the hot cross bun. When her breath hit his fingers she swore she heard him muffle a moan. Lillith nibbled at the cake and smacked her lips together, releasing his hands slowly. With it went the warmth – his warmth, and it saddened her deeply. "Delicious."

"I agree," he said in a low, sultry voice.

When Lillith looked back up at Blaze he was staring at her and not the small cake in his hand. She felt the blush rise to her cheeks and she smiled. Then she quickly let her gaze drop to the ground.

Why did such little actions from Blaze cause such a huge reaction within her? Her heart was beating out of her chest, and it was from the simple fact that they'd shared some food and she'd held his hands. Why did she like it all so much?

"I adore spices, so I make sure my cooks put in plenty of cinnamon, allspice, and nutmeg," Blaze explained. "Not to mention, extra currants too."

"Yes." As her tongue ran over her lips, catching the crumbs, she watched his eyes settle on her mouth. "I adore spice in everything," she told him.

She saw him smile in return, and realized that what she'd just said could be taken in a sexual manner. Lillith was about to correct herself, but decided to let it be. After all, what harm could come from a little flirting?

A thought ran through her overactive mind that he might try to kiss her again, since he was staring so intently at her lips. But they were in the middle of a crowded kitchen with servants all around them, so she knew it was inappropriate even to imagine it right now.

"My lady, my lady, come quickly," came a male voice from behind her. She turned to find Milo walking up with Orvyn. Seeing these two together seemed like trouble to her since neither of them could keep their mouths shut.

"Milo? What's wrong?" asked Lillith, feeling suddenly panicked.

"Your sister has stepped on a turnip and twisted her ankle. She fell to the ground and is in a lot of pain."

"What?" Blaze darted out the door before Lillith could even answer. By the time she got out to the great hall, Blaze was already helping Serena to stand.

"My foot hurts. I think my ankle's broken," wailed Serena in her never-ending act of dramatics.

"My lady, are you all right?" Posy stood there wringing her hands together.

"I'll take a look at it," said Minerva, pushing her way to the front of the crowd. "Blaze, help her up to your solar and put her on the bed."

"Mother, I hardly think that is appropriate," said Blaze.

"Nonsense. There is more room there for me to work. I'll get my healing bag and meet you there." She hurried away.

"Come on," said Blaze. But as soon as they took one step, Serena cried out and grabbed on to him to keep from falling.

"I don't think I can walk. It hurts too much," wailed Lillith's sister.

Lillith rolled her eyes, knowing Serena was probably fine but just wanted the attention. However, it surprised her that she was no longer trying to get away from Blaze. Instead, she almost seemed to be trying to get closer to him.

"I'll carry you," said Blaze, sweeping Serena off her feet. Serena cried out in surprise, and quickly latched her arms around his neck.

"Thank you," she said, smiling at him. Her face was very close to Blaze's and it caused a knot to form in Lillith's stomach.

Lillith followed along silently as Blaze walked to his solar and gently laid Serena on his bed. Minerva rushed in, followed by Posy.

"Let me see your ankle," said Minerva pushing between Blaze

and Lillith, placing her medicine bag on the bed. "Mmm," she said, touching it.

"Ouch!" cried Serena, pushing up to her elbows.

"It is very swollen, but not broken." Minerva opened her bag, pulling out several vials and a rolled-up piece of cloth.

"What are you going to do?" asked Serena.

"My mother is skilled in healing," Blaze told her.

"Using what? A spell?"

"Serena, stop it." Lillith sat down on the edge of the bed. "Minerva uses herbs and items from the earth to heal. She has gemstones like this one she gave me that help to absorb physical and mental pain." She held up her crystal pendant to show her sister.

"My mother gave you that?" Blaze didn't sound happy.

"Yes," she said. "Don't you have one too?"

He was silent and didn't answer.

"Lady Serena doesn't want anything that is not something a normal healer would use," Posy spoke up.

"Oh, you mean I shouldn't use bat wings and lizard tongue and frog eyes to heal her ankle?" asked Minerva, digging through her bag, sounding serious. "That's exactly what I was planning to use." When no one said a word, Minerva looked up and smiled. "I'm jesting," she said.

Still, no one answered.

"Serena, you'll need to remove your stockings so I can put ointment on your ankle and wrap it." Minerva unwound the rolled-up rag.

"I'll leave." Blaze headed to the door. "I'll send a man to carry you to your own bedchamber in a little while."

"You're not going to do it?"

If Lillith wasn't mistaken, Serena sounded as if she were starting to become smitten with Blaze and she didn't like that in the least.

"I'm sorry, but I have things to tend to and preparations to make for All Hallows' Eve that are not finished," Blaze told her.

"Posy, you'll need to stay with Serena," said Lillith, following Blaze to the door.

"I don't want to miss the festivities," complained Serena.

"Well, you're going to have to, I'm afraid," Minerva told her. "If you stay off your foot for a few days, you should be fine."

"Yes, Serena. Listen to Lady Minerva and you will be healed in no time." Lillith left the room, trying to catch up to Blaze.

"Serena is starting to accept me," said Blaze as they walked together.

"Yes. It seems so."

"Does that bother you?"

"Why should it?"

Blaze stopped in his tracks and turned to face her. "Lilly, even if Serena likes me now, I still can't marry her."

"You have to, Blaze. So much depends on this alliance. Without it, there is so much at stake."

"I'm sorry, but I guess I'll just have to find some other way."

He walked off, making Lillith wonder exactly what he meant. Then, she wondered if she really wanted to know.

Fifteen

ALL HALLOWS' Eve came quickly, and Blaze wasn't exactly sure how he felt about it. He'd agreed to join his mother in the stone circle just before midnight to celebrate Samhain as well. He hadn't told Lillith or anyone else, because he didn't want word getting out that he was partaking in a pagan tradition.

Lillith had become very curious, asking him more about Samhain earlier. She'd even asked him if he could do magic. He shook his head as he headed through the courtyard, not believing that she thought he could really do something like that. Actually, he had a weak moment and almost told her to join them in the stone circle tonight, but luckily caught himself in time and didn't invite her. She didn't need to be there. It could only bring trouble.

Blaze stopped in his tracks when he saw Lillith in the courtyard wearing that purple gown again, that made her look so elegant. Her laughter filled the air and soothed his soul. She knelt right on the ground with her hands behind her back, using a bucket of water to show the children how they'd be bobbing for apples later.

One apple floated atop the water. Lillith opened her mouth wide, taking only two tries to grasp it in her teeth. She jumped up and held it in the air in triumph, making all the children giggle.

Blaze clapped slowly, watching her turn toward him, her smile still staining his soul. Soon, he would never see that smile again.

"Blaze. How long have you been standing there?" She swiped a wet strand of hair to the side and took a big bite of the apple.

"Long enough to know you are talented with your mouth." He groaned, realizing exactly how that must sound. "I meant with grabbing things in your teeth. I mean . . . with apples," he said, feeling like he wanted to kill himself right now for being so careless with his words.

She giggled and came over to join him. "Want a bite?" She licked the juices from her lips – an enticing and alluring action, even if she wasn't doing it on purpose.

"Oh, did you mean the apple?"

They both chuckled at that.

"I want a bite of the apple," said a little girl, tugging at her gown.

"Here you go, Eloise." Lillith handed the girl the apple. Several other children gathered around her. "Share with your friends, and don't forget it is almost time to put on your costumes."

The children ran off squealing with excitement.

"Costumes? They don't have any, Lillith."

"Oh, yes they do," she said, reaching into a leather bag she wore over her shoulder. "Your mother and I made lots of masks last night. We also made hoods that have ears like different animals on them for the children to wear when they go souling. Serena and Posy helped us and it went fast. Here is one for you."

Blaze's eyes fastened on the mask that dangled from her fingers. It was purple and black.

"I don't need it."

"Oh, Blaze, you must wear it. Look. It matches mine." She held up another one just like it.

"Nay, Lilly Bee. I appreciate it, but I'm lord of the manor and can't be wearing a mask."

"Just take it," she said. "Mayhap you can wear it later. I mean, if you celebrate Samhain."

"What?" His head snapped up and he wondered if his mother had told her they were meeting with the coven at the stone circle later. "What do you mean?"

"I just thought you might want it, that's all."

Her smile started to disappear and Blaze didn't want her to be sad. "I'll hold on to it for now, but I can't promise I'll wear it." He took the mask and shoved it into his pocket. Lillith was smiling once again.

"My lord, the villagers are approaching for soul cakes," said Emery, joining them.

"Let them in. Have the cooks bring the soul cakes out into the courtyard." said Blaze.

"Aye, my lord."

Blaze noticed Orvyn talking to one of the villagers. The man handed him what looked like a folded-up parchment and left. Orvyn looked up and saw Blaze watching him. He shoved the missive in his pocket and hurried back to the stables.

"Will that be all, my lord?" asked Emery, pulling Blaze's attention back.

"Are all the trestle tables set up?" he asked, looking around the courtyard. He decided to have the feast outdoors so there would be more room for visitors to join them.

"We're just finishing up," Emery answered.

"Good. Invite all our visitors as well as the villagers and those who work at the manor to join in the feast. We've had a prosperous harvest this year and I'd like to share it with them. I have had the cooks prepare plenty of pork, chicken, root vegetables, and even sweetmeats for our guests."

"And don't forget the Barmbrack," called out Minerva, walking from the stables with Milo and Orvyn. The three stopped in front of Blaze.

"What is Barmbrack?" asked Lillith. "I don't think I'm familiar with that dish."

"You'll see," said Blaze.

"It's an old Celtic recipe," explained Minerva. "It is always eaten during Sam- . . . I mean, this time of year." Minerva almost said Samhain again, and Blaze was glad she stopped herself from doing so. Tonight was all about All Hallows' Eve, and he wanted to keep it that way.

"I have a wagon filled with hay to give rides around the orchard," said Orvyn.

"Orvyn, I have seen you lately exchanging things with one of the village men."

"My lord?" asked Orvyn, seeming extremely uncomfortable.

"What did that man from the village just give you?" asked Blaze. "It looked like some sort of missive."

"I – it was nothing, Lord Blaze."

"You have a sweetheart in the village, don't you?" asked Milo, teasing him. "I've noticed too. You're sending love notes back and forth, aren't you?"

"I'd rather not say." Orvyn looked down at the ground.

Blaze decided it was doing no harm and he didn't want to ruin the celebration. He would let it go for now and ask Orvyn more about it in a few days.

"Carry on," said Blaze.

"I'll drive the children in the hay wagon. Can I drive it? Please?" asked Milo anxiously.

"Sure. Why not," mumbled Blaze, not really caring. "Just stay near the manor and don't go out into the woods tonight," he added, not wanting Milo to show up with a wagonful of people at the stone circle later.

"Aye, my lord." Milo and Orvyn walked off discussing what path the wagon ride should take.

"What's the matter, Blaze?" asked Minerva. "You seem worried."

He hadn't had time yet to ask Milo not to say anything about the stone circle. Hopefully, with all the excitement of the festivities, the boy would forget about it for now.

"Nothing," said Blaze.

"If you're worried about Milo having seen the stone circle and telling others, don't be," said Lillith. "I've asked him to keep it to himself."

"Thank you," said Blaze, never thinking it would be Lillith who was helping to keep a secret such as this.

"Excuse me, my lord," said Barnaby, interrupting. "The head cook says the food is ready."

"Fine. Everyone, please take a seat. Lillith, you'll join Mother and me at the dais they've constructed in the courtyard."

Blaze's raven flew down and Blaze held out his arm for a perch. It landed with stealth and grace.

"I think Ebony is hungry too," said Lillith.

"She's a beggar. Don't give her a thing. She can find her own food. Go on, now," said Blaze, jerking his arm and sending the bird back up into the sky.

Minerva's cat shot between Blaze's legs next, almost causing him to fall.

"Damn it," he spat. "Mother, can't you keep that thing in your chamber?"

"No, I can't," said Minerva. "And be careful not to step on Sam."

As they headed for the table, Lillith realized that Blaze seemed shaken.

"Do cats bother you that much?" she asked.

"Only when black cats run between my legs on Samhain," he grumbled. "I'm going to have bad luck now."

"That's a myth and you know it, Blaze," scolded Minerva, bending down and picking up the cat which yowled and swiped out its paw in the air. "Although I must say something is upsetting my familiar. I think he knows the dead come back to life tonight."

"That's not true. Is it?" asked Lillith, suddenly feeling scared.

"Anything is possible," said Minerva. "Oh, Lady Lillith, you'll sit here next to me," said Minerva as they walked up to the dais.

Lillith looked around and saw way too many settings for just the three of them. "Who are all the extra plates for?" she asked.

"Well, one was for Serena, but she's up in her room," said Minerva. "The other two are for your father and brother."

"What?" Lillith's heart jumped and her body stiffened. "Lady Minerva, they're not coming. They're dead."

"I know. But after all, it is custom to set places for the dead tonight."

All this talk started to spook Lillith. She felt as if she wanted her sister by her for comfort.

"Blaze, I think Serena should be here. Can you go get her?" she asked.

Blaze was about to sit. "What? Why?"

"She didn't want to miss the celebration. Besides, she has to eat."

"And she is your betrothed, Blaze," said Minerva.

"Not for long," he mumbled.

Minerva put her cat down on the table. "Son, I agree with Lady Lillith. It would be good for appearances if your bride-to-be was here as well. Now, go get her."

"If it'll stop you two from hounding me so I can eat my meal in peace, then I will."

He headed away, leaving Minerva and Lillith by themselves.

"Is there anything you'd like to ask me, my dear?" Minerva picked up a goblet with some spiced wine and took a sip. Sam inspected the items on the table, rubbing up against them.

Lillith had a lot of questions about witches and Samhain and even Blaze. However, seeing those empty places at the end of table for the dead spooked her so much that she couldn't even think of a thing to say.

"Nay," she said, taking a goblet of wine from the cupbearer and chugging down the liquid. Something felt odd but she couldn't put her finger on what it was. Nightfall would be closing in fast. With the loss of light, spirits from the other side might start to emerge, just as the myths said. As much as Lillith would love to see her father and brother again, the thought of them showing up in spirit form made her very uncomfortable. Lillith had been so excited about these festivities, but now, she couldn't wait until All Hallows' Eve was over.

Once Serena joined Lillith at the table, she immediately felt better. It wasn't easy watching Blaze carry her to the table, when all Lillith could think about was herself being in Blaze's arms. Still, they enjoyed the meal, and handed out soul cakes to the beggars and children who approached the dais, promising a prayer for a dead one in exchange for the small bun.

"Thank you for suggesting I join you," said Serena, finishing up her meal.

"I wish Father and Robert were really here with us." Lillith glanced down the table once more to the places that were set for them. There was actually food on the plates now, and that was eerie.

"Don't you think it's a little scary, setting plates of food at the table for the dead?" asked Serena in a whisper.

"I do," Lillith whispered back. "It's not like the ghosts are really going to eat."

The meal continued, and a little while later, Lillith looked back to the places set for the dead and gasped.

"Serena," said Lillith. "Look. The food is gone at the place settings they put out for Father and Robert."

Serena looked down the table and her eyes opened wide. "You're right. Oh, Lillith, I'm scared. I don't want to see any spirits tonight."

"Neither do I."

They both jerked backward when the cat named Sam jumped atop the table right in front of them, looking for scraps. Lillith noticed food on the cat's whiskers as well as his huge belly. She realized now who had eaten from the ghostly settings.

"Sam, you've been a bad boy, haven't you?" she asked, running her hand over the cat's head, letting out a sigh of relief.

Then Blaze's raven swooped down toward the cat, scaring it. Sam hissed and arched his back. The raven shrieked, turning and diving down at the cat once more, causing gooseflesh to appear on Lillith's arms.

"Off the table! Both of you," Blaze shouted, waving his arms in the air until both the cat and raven left.

"My lord," interrupted one of Blaze's guards. "The pageboy is ready to take the children for a ride in the wagon, but is waiting for Orvyn."

"Well, where the hell is my stablemaster?" asked Blaze.

"I'm not sure, my lord. No one can seem to find him."

"Oh, there he is," said Serena, pointing to the front gate. Orvyn was leading a horse, heading for the gate.

"Orvyn, where are you going?" Blaze shouted across the courtyard. "Get back to work. Now."

"Aye, my lord," said Orvyn with a nod, bringing the horse back to the stable.

"Orvyn has been acting odd lately," Blaze said aloud.

"Mayhap he was sneaking off to see a sweetheart, like Milo said." Lillith pushed her empty plate away and a servant scooped it off the table.

"It seems if he had a sweetheart in the village, she'd be here since I invited everyone to the celebration," said Blaze. "I'll have to talk to him."

"Oh, Blaze, let Orvyn have his secrets. Don't bother him about it. He is not causing any trouble," said Minerva, not seeming at all concerned.

"Mayhap you're right," Blaze mumbled.

"Oh, here comes the Barmbrack." Minerva instructed the servers to give a big piece of the cake to everyone at the dais.

"This looks good," said Serena, inspecting the sweet treat.

"I'm not hungry. Someone can have mine," answered Lillith, too full from the meal.

"You're not going to eat it?" asked Minerva.

"I don't think so," answered Lillith.

"But it's tradition, my dear. You have to. It might be a good omen for your future."

"What do you mean?" asked Lillith.

"There are objects hidden in the cake," Blaze explained. "Depending on what you might find, means different things."

"Like what?" she asked.

"Well," said Blaze, "for example, if you find a piece of cloth in your cake, it means you'll have hardships, and a stick denotes a bad marriage."

"What?" gasped Lillith. "Why would I want to know either of those?" She was already distraught enough about having to marry the baron. She didn't need a stupid stick telling her that her marriage would be awful.

"Plus, finding a pea means you won't marry at all this year," added Minerva.

"That one might not be so bad," she said under her breath, still not seeing the point of this game.

"Blaze, don't just tell them the bad things," scolded his mother. "There are good objects and lucky ones to find, too."

"Like what?" asked Serena, picking up her spoon.

"Such as, if you find a coin you will be wealthy. And if you find a ring you will be married this year."

I already know the answers to all those things," said Lillith, pushing her plate with the cake away from her.

"Well, I want to know," said Serena, digging into the cake eagerly. "Oh! I found something," she shouted, holding up a coin. "I'm going to be rich."

"We already have plenty of money, Serena. That doesn't mean a thing," commented Lillith.

"Lord Blaze, check your cake," said Serena excitedly. "See what your future holds."

"I do like the taste of it, but I'm not looking for objects." He dug into his cake anyway, but there was nothing but fruit inside.

"Mother, your turn to try it," said Blaze.

"Why not?" Minerva dug into her cake and scowled. "A pea," she said, sounding sorely disappointed, holding it up in two fingers. "I guess I won't marry this year."

"And neither should you," said Blaze, taking another big bite of cake. "Father just died and you are in mourning."

"Sister, you try it." Serena urged Lillith to get involved in the game.

"I don't care about it, Serena and I'm not hungry," said Lillith.

"Lilly, I've never known you to be a bad sport," said Blaze.

"All right," she finally agreed, using her spoon to dig into the cake. She hit something hard immediately, and picked it up.

"It's a ring!" cried Serena. "It means you will marry."

"We already know I'm getting married this year since I'm betrothed, so this means nothing." Lillith threw it down on the table. Blaze picked it up and wiped the cake off of it, with a hand cloth.

"It looks like your marriage to the baron will be a happy one after all, Lilly. Congratulations," he said, most likely just trying to be polite.

Since she was sitting next to Blaze, he took her hand and slid the toy ring made of tin onto her finger.

Lillith looked up into Blaze's eyes as he held her hand and her heart almost melted. She felt as if she were marrying him and he just put the wedding ring on her finger. She couldn't break the connection between them and neither could he. He felt something too. She knew he did, even though neither of them said a word about it.

"Oh, Lillith, they're lighting the bonfire," said Serena excitedly. "I want to go over there. Can someone take me?"

Blaze let go of Lillith's hand and stood. "Of course, my lady. I'd be happy to carry you over to a chair by the bonfire."

Lillith was left staring at her hand as Blaze carried Serena over to the bonfire. Serena giggled and clung to Blaze's neck. It seemed that Lillith's sister was no longer frightened of him, and she seemed to like the attention she was getting as he carried her everywhere she went, even though Lillith wasn't convinced she couldn't walk on her own. If they kept getting along so well, Lillith was afraid they would go through with the wedding after all.

She stared at the toy ring on her finger once more, tears quickly filling her eyes.

"My dear." Minerva walked over and placed her hand on Lillith's shoulder. "Come with me."

Lillith wiped away a tear and stood, following Minerva.

Looking back over her shoulder once more, Lillith saw her sister once again in Blaze's arms. Any hopes regarding Blaze being her husband someday diminished quickly. Now, every last dream of Lillith's shattered.

* * *

Lillith followed Minerva into Blaze's solar, surprised to see her cards stacked up on the table. Minerva lit a candle as well as some incense. If Lillith wasn't mistaken, it smelled like sage. Then the woman brought a bowl of salt to the table, as well as a handful of gemstones and laid them down.

"What's all this?" asked Lillith, standing in the doorway, not sure if she should enter. After all, it was All Hallows' Eve, the woman was a witch, and everything about this setting looked pagan to her.

"Come in, my dear. Don't be frightened." Minerva walked over and closed the door behind her.

"I'm not frightened." Lillith slowly approached the table. "I'm just . . . intrigued, that's all." She reached out to touch the cards, but Minerva swooped in and scooped them up and sat down on a chair.

"Sit," she instructed, nodding to the chair across from her.

"I'm going to read the cards for you. However, we'd better do it fast, before Blaze returns. He still doesn't like when I do this."

"Why do you do it in his solar then, instead of your own chamber?" asked Lillith, sitting down atop the chair.

"The vibrations are better in here. Plus, this is probably the last place he'd think of looking for me," Minerva answered with a smile. "Are you ready, my dear?"

"I – I'm not sure. After all, you said Blaze won't like it."

"I'm doing this for him. For you. For both of you." She leaned forward and smiled. "I know you two are in love. Now, don't you want to see if you'll end up together?" She shuffled the cards and then pushed the deck over to Lillith. "Cut the deck, please. The cards need for you to touch them."

"This won't matter in the least," said Lillith, cutting the deck of cards. "After all, I already know my future. I'm betrothed to the baron and I will never be able to marry Blaze."

"Things don't always turn out the way you think." Minerva stacked the deck again and then dealt a few cards. She turned the first one over, and then the next. "Oh my," she said, studying the cards, not sounding too enthusiastic or happy.

"What is it?" Curiosity got the best of Lillith. She leaned forward to see the cards. One of them was the Lovers. Two naked people were embraced in each other's arms. There was a mountain behind them and a bright sun above them. She didn't think that was a bad thing, but had never had a real card reading before. She and Blaze had played with these cards once as children, and they had frightened her out of her mind. Why was she even in here, she started to wonder?

"I see love in your life with a man with dark hair," said Minerva, taking a deep breath and then releasing it.

"The baron has dark hair," Lillith told her.

"So does my son," answered the woman. "Turn over the next one, dear."

"Well . . . all right." Lillith decided this wasn't so bad after all. Mayhap it would restore her hope, even if it was false hope. Her hand shook as she reached out and turned over the next card. "The ten of wands? What does that mean?" She inspected the card of a man carrying a bunch of staves, unable to handle them all.

"It means you have the weight of the world on your shoulders, or possibly that you have entered into a situation and are in over your head."

"Oh," she said. "That sounds about right." This wasn't telling her anything about her life that she didn't already know. Neither was it saying anything other than she would end up marrying the baron. She flipped over the next card and heard Minerva gasp.

"What? What is it?" Lillith needed to know.

The card was the three of swords. Three swords were stuck into a heart with blood dripping down. It made her swallow hard. "This can't be good," she mumbled, swishing away smoke from the sage that was clouding up her eyes. "Please, tell me what it means."

Minerva hesitated, reached into the bowl of salt, and threw some right into Lillith's face.

"Oh!" cried, Lillith, wiping the granules off her cheeks, tasting salt on her lips. "What was that for?"

"Salt is a form of protection," said Minerva. "You can never be too cleansed."

"This card means something bad, doesn't it?" asked Lillith.

"Well, I won't lie, it does mean heartbreak, sorrow and pain."

"Oh." All the air left Lillith's lungs. She didn't need to hear this.

"However, it also means it won't last. Better things are on the horizon. You just need to let go of your emotions -let go of the past and move on."

"Oh," said Lillith, realizing this meant she had to let go of Blaze, but she didn't know if she could do it.

Minerva flipped over the next card, and Lillith realized the woman was not smiling. Minerva's mouth turned down into a frown. Lillith could barely bring herself to look at the card. The card was the devil with a naked man and woman chained to it.

"I don't like this one," Lillith mumbled.

"It signifies poison in a relationship," said Minerva. "As well as desire, shamelessness, and being reckless."

Lillith thought about the kisses and caresses she'd shared with Blaze lately, even though he was betrothed to her sister. Part of her was ashamed by the way she'd acted. She'd let her emotions get out of control, and she hadn't acted like a proper lady at all. She supposed she was being reckless, just like the cards said.

"What's this one?" she asked, reaching for the last card.

Minerva's hand shot out and grabbed her wrist, stopping her from turning it over. "It doesn't matter, my dear. The cards aren't always right. I suggest we go join the others now. The apple bobbing is taking place and the costume parade around the bonfire will be starting. We should go." Minerva started to scoop up the cards, but Lillith slapped her hand down over the uncovered card.

"Not yet," said Lillith, sliding the card toward her. "I want you to finish my reading first."

"I get the feeling we should stop," protested Minerva, but Lillith didn't heed the warning. She flipped the card over and immediately wished she had listened to Minerva after all. Her body froze. Lillith found herself staring at the death card – the last card she ever wanted to see, especially on a night like this.

"Am I g-going to die?" she whispered, suddenly feeling very frightened.

"The death card doesn't always mean a physical death," explained Minerva. "It could be death of a relationship, or a way of living, or –"

The door burst open and Blaze entered the room with Orvyn following on his heels. They stopped in their tracks when they saw the women. "Mother? Lilly? What's going on here?" growled Blaze.

"Are those fortune-telling cards?" asked Orvyn with wide eyes.

"We were just leaving," said Minerva, gathering up the cards and quickly blowing out the candle. She picked up some salt in her fingers and threw it at Lilly once more and then dropped some on the table as well before she snuffed out the incense.

"You really are witches, just like the rumors said." Orvyn walked over to the table to get a better look at what was going on.

Blaze could have died on the spot. He had brought Orvyn to his solar to ask him about his secrecy with the villagers lately, but never expected to find his mother and Lillith here, doing this! The last thing he needed was Orvyn finding out for sure that his mother was a witch. Now, Orvyn would think Lillith was one too. This was not going to fare well for her at all. For none of them, actually.

"Nay, it's not what you think," Blaze told Orvyn, not exactly knowing how to explain this.

"I always wondered about those cards. Can I see them?" Orvyn stretched his neck.

"Nay! Now, go to the stable and check the horses and see to the apple bobbing," Blaze told Orvyn with a finger pointing to the door.

"Yes, my lord, but I thought you wanted to speak to me about something."

"Not now. We'll talk later. It can wait."

Orvyn seemed disappointed, but turned to leave.

"Wait, Orvyn," said Blaze.

"Yes, my lord?" He turned back around.

"In a few days when the festivities are over, you and I will have a talk about what you just saw. But for now, for tonight, just please keep quiet about any ideas you have regarding anything you have seen here today."

"Of course, my lord," said Orvyn with a bow, leaving and closing the door behind him.

As soon as he was gone, Blaze exploded with anger.

"Mother! How could you? And Lillith? What is the matter with you two? Don't you two realize what you've just done? Orvyn can't keep his mouth shut. This is going to blow up in all our faces." He paced the room and shook his head. "And just when I thought things might turn out all right. Now I'm doomed. Doomed! And it's all your fault." He glared at both the women.

"I'm sorry," said Lillith, wiping a tear from her eye. "I was just curious, but now I wish that I had never come up here at all."

"It was my fault," interrupted Minerva. "I wanted to do a reading for her."

"Whatever for?" growled Blaze.

"She did it for us, Blaze," said Lillith, her voice quaking. "She wanted to find out if we'll end up together."

"What?" asked Blaze, wondering now if there was possibly a way to make this happen. "Well, what did you find out?"

Lillith bit her lip and looked like she was trying to keep from crying. She wound the end of her hair around her fingers, and got up from the table so quickly that she knocked into it, causing a card to fall to the floor. Blaze walked over and picked it up.

"The fool," he said, handing the card to his mother.

"I've been a fool to hope that we could possibly end up together, Blaze. But now I know that it will never happen." Lillith ran for the door.

"Lilly, wait," he called out, but when he started to go after her, his mother stopped him.

"Leave her be, Blaze," she said in a low voice. "The reading wasn't a good one. I know now that I never should have suggested it. I'm sorry."

Once again, his mother was creating havoc in his life and Blaze was more than tired of it.

"Mother, first you start a feud and now you ruin the hopes of the woman I love."

"I didn't start that feud and you know it. And there was no hope for you and Lillith before I even got home, so don't go blaming that on me."

"This has got to end. I can't live a life of constantly trying to protect your secrets."

"Our secrets, Blaze," said his mother.

"Nay." He furiously shook his head. "I am not going to be a part of all your crazy ways. Not any longer."

"Mayhap I can read the cards for you. That might tell us what we can do about all this."

"Nay," he answered, shaking his head. "I've had enough of your card readings. Look how upset you made Lillith."

"Now, Blaze, she just took the reading the wrong way."

"So, it wasn't bad, then?"

"Well . . . I wouldn't say it was uplifting. But, of course, these things can be interpreted in many different ways."

"My lord?" There was knock at the door. "My lord, the bonfire is lit. Did you want to have the musicians play music for the costume parade?" asked his steward.

"Yes, Barnaby, I'll be right there," Blaze called out. Then, turning back to his mother, he shook his head. "If Lillith is scarred for life now, I blame you for it," he told her.

"I didn't do anything," she protested.

"You most certainly did. You took away that girl's last and only hope that things might turn out the way she'd like them to. That is the worst thing anyone can ever do to a person who is so distraught."

Without waiting for her to answer, Blaze turned and left the room, trying to gather himself so no one would see just how upset and unsettled he was right now. By the looks of things, his hope was gone now too. There was no more doubt in his mind. Lilly and he would never end up together.

Sixteen

THIS WHOLE NIGHT was naught but a blur for Blaze. He had a hard time focusing on anything but Lillith. She was being the perfect hostess, seeing to all the guests and their children who came calling. Even after the card reading she'd just had, she still managed to hold her head high and acted as if nothing was wrong. Lillith was a strong woman, and Blaze admired that about her.

The children even convinced Lillith to bob for apples along with them. She dunked her entire face into the water like he'd seen her do before. It took her several tries, but she easily came up with an apple clamped in her teeth.

Even with the witchy gown she wore, Blaze's heart went out to her. She was trying so hard to fit in to his family. He wanted that more than anything. She had even seemed to befriend his mother, which, in his opinion, was not an easy thing for anyone to do.

Lillith was wonderful with the children. He realized she would make a terrific mother, wife, and also a perfect lady of the castle someday. Sadly, it wouldn't be here and with him.

He envied the lucky Sir Edward Bancroft who was getting her as his wife. Blaze supposed the betrothal to the baron was a smart match for Lillith's family. After all, she would have everything she needed or wanted. That was something Blaze could never give her.

He cursed inwardly, wishing he hadn't even seen those stupid cards tonight. It was evident now that every hope was gone and there was no way that he and Lillith would end up together. He felt just like that fool on the card he'd picked up. Before all hope had diminished, he thought if he broke off the betrothal with Serena, something might happen that he could still have a chance of marrying Lillith. Nothing but a fool's dream, is what it was.

"Damn it," he spat, kicking at a pebble. He'd caught a glimpse of the horrible death card in Lillith's reading as well. It was the card he hated the most in that blasted deck. It was also the last one he wanted to see tonight. The more he thought about those blasted cards, the angrier he became. Sam, his mother's cat, sat down in front of him and meowed.

"Get out of here," he said, thinking this bad luck was brought on by the cat crossing between his legs earlier.

His mother was busy helping to light the lanterns, since it was now dusk. Candles were placed inside the hollowed-out turnips, and the faces carved in them glowed. The parade was about to start. This was the night that the dead could supposedly come back to life. The thought terrified the children and made them stay close to their parents. He, on the other hand, didn't believe this silly superstition for one minute. However, after seeing that death card tonight, part of him feared that someone was going to die.

He had to stop that from happening. If Lillith died, he wouldn't know how to go on without her. Blaze would also blame himself. He should have burned those damned cards long ago, but didn't want to upset his mother. Now, he no longer cared. Since his mother was distracted and so was Lillith, he figured it would be the best time to stop this problem and keep it from ever happening again.

He stormed off to his solar to get the cards. He'd be able to throw them into the bonfire before everyone gathered around.

Yes, he decided, by burning the cards mayhap he'd somehow change the events of the future that were predicted for his sweet little Lilly Bee.

Blaze approached his room, making a beeline to the deck of cards, still sitting on his table. Scooping them up, he turned to go, but stopped. He had the feeling someone or something was watching him. The room was dark, but the window was open and the light from the full moon spilled into the room.

"Don't let her go, Blaze," he heard someone whisper from over by the door. He spun around, and for a brief second, he swore he saw his father standing there in a long cloak, but then the vision disappeared. Blaze shook his head, thinking he was going mad.

He left the room, quickly heading over to the bonfire. When no one was looking, he tossed the deck of cards into the flames, glad to see them burn.

"Lord Blaze, what was that you tossed into the fire?"

He turned around to see Orvyn standing there in a long cape watching him.

"Nothing," he said with a shrug. "Were you just inside the keep, Orvyn? Up by my solar, by any chance?"

"Nay, my lord. Why would I be there when the festivities are here in the courtyard? If you'll excuse me, I need to lead the parade. The children are anxiously waiting."

"Of course," said Blaze with a slight nod.

"Oh, look," said Milo approaching the bonfire. "It looks like something fell in by accident. I'll scoop it out, my lord, before it burns."

"Leave it," Blaze commanded, with an outstretched arm to keep him from getting any closer.

"But someone might have lost something important," said Milo.

"Believe me, it's nothing important. Now, go help Orvyn with the parade. Just keep everyone inside the courtyard since it is already dark."

"Aye, my lord," answered Milo, looking back at the fire once again. "When does the veil to the other world open up? I can't wait to see which of the dead come through."

"How the hell should I know?" Blaze stormed away, not wanting to talk to anyone right now. All Hallows' Eve was never a favorite holiday of his. And for some reason, he had the feeling that by the end of the night, he was going to hate it even more.

Seventeen

"HERE I GO," said Serena, sitting with her back to the fire. She took a hazelnut in her hand, made a face and then tossed the nut over her shoulder into the fire. "Did it pop?" she asked Lillith, hurriedly turning around to look. "I can't see it." She stretched her neck, looking for it in the fire. "Did it pop or burn, Lillith? I need to know."

"What does it matter?" Lillith answered, feeling anxious yet disheartened at the same time.

"You know why she's asking," said the handmaid, Posy. "If it pops, it means the man she was thinking about loves her. If it burns, it means there is no hope."

"Let me look." Lillith saw the hazelnut burning. "I'm sorry, sister. It didn't pop."

"Oh," Serena answered, looking discouraged.

"Who were you thinking about?" asked Lillith.

"No one," Serena answered quickly, making Lillith wonder if she was thinking about Blaze.

"Well, I'm sorry, but it doesn't look like your mystery man loves you after all," Lillith told her.

"You try," said Serena, pushing a hazelnut into Lillith's hand.

"Nay. There is no reason for me to do this. It doesn't matter anymore." Lillith gave the hazelnut back, not needing any more bad news today.

"Then throw apple peels over your shoulder to see the initial of the man you'll marry." Serena pushed an apple and a knife into Lillith's hands.

"Fine," said Lillith with a sigh, only doing it to stop her sister from bothering her. She peeled the apple and threw the long peel over her shoulder.

"It's looks like the letter B," said Posy, inspecting it.

"B? Like Blaze?" asked Serena.

"No," Lillith answered. "B as in baron or Baron of Bancroft. B as in betrothed. So, there you see, my future is set."

"At least try taking a bite of apple and combing your hair while you look into a shiny platter," continued Serena. "It is said you'll see the man you will marry in the fire."

Lillith realized her sister wasn't going to let her stop until she tried every last one of these stupid All Hallows' Eve superstitious customs.

"This is the last one," she said, taking the brush Serena handed her, and then a bite of the apple she'd just peeled.

"Posy, give her the platter," said Serena. "Don't forget to look into the platter for the reflection of your husband."

"Serena, we both know whom we're marrying so this is naught but a childish game that means nothing at all," Lillith told her.

"I think it is the work of the devil," complained Posy, still handing the shiny platter to Lillith anyway. "I don't like being a part of these evil things."

"Evil things? That's a little harsh," said Lillith, giving Posy the apple and taking the platter from her. "These customs are silly, but can't hurt anyone," she assured her handmaid.

"Well, I, for one, pity your sister," said Posy. "No one should have to marry a warlock. It just isn't right."

"Posy, I've changed my mind about Lord Blaze," said Serena. "I think he is rather nice, actually."

"You do?" asked Lillith, not wanting to hear this for some reason.

"Yes," she answered with a smile. "I think mayhap I'll get used to being his wife after all."

"Hmph," snorted Posy. "He's got both of you bewitched now."

"Hold up the platter, Lillith, and look at the reflection to see the man you'll marry in the flames behind you." Serena was a child at times, always wanting to play games that Lillith didn't care about at all. Especially games involving love and husbands that didn't even pertain to either of them anymore.

"You do realize that I'm only doing this to get you off my back," said Lillith in frustration.

Holding the platter in front of her, Lillith stood with her back to the fire. "I wish to see my lover," she said, looking at the reflection in the shiny platter. She saw herself, of course. But then, behind her in the reflection, she thought she saw what looked like a man with dark hair. It really worked! Spinning around, she looked at the bonfire, expecting to see a wispy vision of the baron. Instead, there, through the flames, she saw Blaze talking with his mother. She gasped.

"Who did you see, Sister?" asked Serena curiously. "Was it the baron?"

"I – I – it didn't work," she said, handing the brush and platter back to her sister. Now, after her sister expressed how excited she was to be marrying Blaze, how could Lillith tell her she saw Blaze in the reflection? And what did any of it really mean? This just proved that it was nothing but a stupid game.

It was nightfall now and the full moon shone down brightly overhead. Everyone seemed to be having a good time around the bonfire and the costume parade was a success. The musicians played a lively tune and some of the people even danced. Everyone drank heartily. The children chased each other around in circles, pretending they were animals, like their costumes depicted.

There was a chill in the air now as the hour approached midnight. The lanterns that were placed all around the courtyard burned with candles inside, some of them already having burned out and having to be relit. Scary faces carved into the turnips seemed to be watching her everywhere she went.

Lillith couldn't stop thinking about her awful card reading and the card of death. That only made her think about the thinning veil between two worlds and spirits possibly coming through. She looked up to the sky, almost expecting to see a ghost, but there was nothing. She had almost convinced herself none of this was true when she felt something brush past her leg that made her jump and cry out.

"There's the kitty," said one of the children, chasing Sam right past her. It took her a minute to calm her racing heart, realizing it was no ghost touching her leg but just Minerva's fat cat who liked to steal food.

This made her feel a little better, but it was almost midnight – the witching hour. This thought sent a shiver up her spine. She felt someone touch her on the shoulder, and jumped again, turning to see someone wearing a mask made of cloth and fur. She screamed.

"Lady Lillith, it's just me," laughed Milo, removing his mask. "My, you are jumpy tonight."

"It's just that it's All Hallows' Eve," she told him.

"It's because the spirits are about to rise from the dead, isn't it?" Milo put his mask back on and raised his hands over his head making ghost noises.

"Stop it," she scolded, feeling chilled, wrapping her cloak tighter around her. She walked away, noticing Blaze and his mother riding horses out of the stable toward the gate of Skull Manor. She hurriedly ran to the stables, wondering where they were going.

"My lady? Is there something you need?" It was Orvyn who

always seemed to appear at the most inopportune times. He wore a costume, like everyone else. His depicted an executioner with a long black robe. He wore a mask over his eyes, and held a farmer's scythe in his hand used for cutting wheat. It was a little scary.

"I need a horse saddled. Quickly," she said, her eyes roaming back to the front gate. She wanted to be with Blaze right now. No matter where he was going, she wanted to be with him.

"I suppose you'll be following Lord Blaze and his mother to the stone circle then?" Orvyn started to saddle a horse.

"What?" she gasped, wondering how he even knew about such a thing. "Stone circle?" She feigned ignorance. "Whatever do you mean?"

"Milo told me he saw it hidden deep in the woods."

"Oh." She groaned inwardly. Milo seemed to like to run at the mouth too.

"It's the witch's circle in the woods. It is where they do their chanting and dancing and sacrificing, especially on a night like this," said Orvyn. "They call it Samhain, but you probably know all about that. It's the pagan's version of All Hallows' Eve."

"I might have heard of it," she said, trying to find out what else Orvyn knew. "What do you know about all this?"

"Well, I believe Lord Blaze is a warlock and his mother is a witch. Just like the rumors say."

"I'm sure you don't know what you're talking about." She mounted the horse, preparing to leave.

"I'll come with you, my lady. To protect you."

"Nay, you won't. I don't need anyone to guard me. I'm in no danger."

"How can you say that? Especially on a night when the dead come back to life?"

"If you're trying to scare me, it won't work." It already had, but she wouldn't admit it.

"I only meant, are you hoping to talk with your brother or your father tonight, my lady?"

That shook her up even more. All she could think of were

those place settings at the table for the spirits of those who had passed on and how empty it made her feel. A shiver ran through her again.

"I don't believe spirits can roam our world, Orvyn. That is naught but stories to scare the children on All Hallows' Eve. Once a person is dead, they are gone. Forever."

"If you insist," said Orvyn with a shrug. "But I've seen ghosts in the past so I know they're real."

"You have?" she gasped. "Where?"

He didn't answer. "Are you sure I can't escort you into the woods? It is a dark night and not one to be travelling alone."

"Nay. The moon is full, and I've got my dagger to protect me. I won't be gone long. Please, don't tell anyone where I went."

"Of course not, my lady."

Lillith headed out the gate, directing her horse toward the stone circle. She needed to see how Blaze and his mother celebrated Samhain. She wanted to know more, and couldn't count on Blaze telling her anything on his own. The farther she went into the woods, the darker it became. She heard the howl of a wolf and looked back over her shoulder.

Her horse became agitated, and she had all she could do to hold it steady. Now, she regretted not taking Orvyn's offer after all. She didn't like being out here in the dark all alone.

"It's all right, girl," she said, rubbing the horse's neck. "There is nothing to be afraid of."

Just as she said that, something flew over her head and she screamed. Then she realized it was Blaze's raven. It landed in a branch overhead, watching her.

"Ebony, you scared me," she spat, feeling her heart beating like a drum about ready to burst from her chest. "Don't you know birds aren't supposed to fly at night? You could break your neck."

The raven squawked and flew off into the night sky.

She heard twigs snapping off to the side, and her head jerked around again. "Who's there?" she called out, but of course, no one answered. All she could think about was Orvyn saying he'd seen the ghosts of dead ones come back. This thought terrified her. Her hand went to her waist to grab her dagger, but to her horror, it wasn't there. She must have dropped it somewhere along the road.

"Oh, nay," she said, not liking the fact she had no way to defend herself now. Then again, if she would be attacked by spirits from the other side of the veil, she didn't think a dagger would do her any good.

She was about to turn around and go back to the manor, when she realized she wore her leather bag over her shoulder. She still had Blaze's dagger with the moons and stars and skull on it, inside the bag. She had never had the chance to return it to him yet since Posy stole it from his chamber.

An owl hooted in the night, sounding so human that it made her skin crawl. Her heart sped up again. The moon was half-hidden behind a cloud now and it was getting even darker. She slid her hand inside the bag, closing her fingers around the hilt of Blaze's dagger. Pulling it out, she held it up in front of her for protection.

When the moon peeked out from behind the clouds, the moonbeams fell upon the metal of the blade, almost seeming to make it glow. She gasped again, wondering if this dagger held some sort of magical power. If she hadn't been afraid for her own safety and needed protection, she would have thrown it down.

Lillith thought she heard music and the snapping of a fire from up ahead. When she peered through the trees, she was sure she saw orange on the branches from a fire burning nearby.

"It must be the stone circle," she said to herself, glad to have finally found it. She dismounted her horse and tied the reins to a tree. Through the woods she could see a group of people, all dressed in costumes, dancing around the bonfire inside the stone circle.

She saw Blaze's back as he stood next to his mother. The

group chanted and someone played flute music. The whole thing was intriguing, yet terrifying at the same time. She couldn't let the witches see her. If they caught her here, there was no telling what they'd do to her.

Looking at the dagger in her hand that led the way, she decided she didn't want them to see that she had this, either. If it was some sort of special or enchanted blade, they would be furious that she had it.

Gripping Blaze's dagger tightly behind her back now, she moved closer, hoping to hear more of what was happening up ahead. Lillith realized it was nearing the midnight hour. And as if being by herself in the woods spying on the witches wasn't frightening enough, she kept thinking of what Milo said about the dead coming back to life. Her heart beat faster and faster. She didn't want to see the dead spirits of her father or brother. She just wanted them to rest in peace.

Lillith felt something or someone touch her shoulder. She screamed and spun around to find two men standing there in costumes and masks.

"Stay back or I'll kill you," she spat, waving Blaze's dagger in the air.

"Calm down. We're not going to hurt you, Lady Lillith." The men removed their masks to show their identities.

"Orvyn? Milo? What are you two doing here?" She let out a breath of relief to know it was them.

"We came to protect you, my lady," said Milo. "Orvyn found your dagger on the ground after you left the manor. You must have dropped it. We figured you needed protection." Milo held both his dagger and hers up in the air to show her. "As soon as Orvyn told me you came to the stone circle, I knew we had to follow."

"Orvyn said that, did he?" She scowled at Orvyn for following her after she said she didn't want him to go with her.

"It was for your own safety, my lady," Orvyn tried to convince her. Somehow, Lillith had the feeling it was much more than that. Orvyn was nosey and most likely wanted to see what was going on in the woods. "Milo knew exactly how to get here, so he showed me the way." He held up a dagger too. "We've come prepared to see to your safety, should you need it."

"Thank you, but I'm quite capable of taking care of myself." She held Blaze's dagger higher.

"Isn't that the blade I saw with blood on it by your father's dead body?" asked Milo with wide eyes.

She lowered it quickly. "Yes. It's Blaze's dagger," she admitted. "However, he was hunting the day he ran across my father. He didn't kill him. Father was already dead."

"My lady, do you really believe that?" asked Milo. "After all . . . Lord Blaze is a warlock, and this proves it." His eyes roamed over to Blaze at the bonfire.

"It proves nothing but the fact that Blaze's family celebrates the holiday in a different way than we do," said Lillith. "There is nothing to fear."

"Not even witches and warlocks?" asked Milo, shaking his head. "They're evil."

"Sometimes, we get the wrong idea of people when they are not like us, but actually they are not that different from us at all. I assure you, we have nothing to worry about here."

Lillith turned back to see one of the warlocks pulling a bleating goat up to the sacrificial altar, and she almost swooned. Mayhap, she was wrong about all this after all.

* * *

Blaze stood at the bonfire in the center of the stone circle, wishing now that he hadn't let his mother convince him to partake in the Samhain tradition after all. He'd only brought her here because he didn't want her riding through the forest at night alone. He never planned on being part of any of this.

"Blaze, you'll make the sacrifice tonight," said his mother. "Where is your dagger? The one with the skull and moons and stars? That's the one you need to use."

"I don't know, Mother. I looked for my dagger earlier in my chamber and couldn't find it. I thought you'd taken it."

"Nay, I don't have it. Oh well, just use mine," she said, handing him her dagger. "I'll say the words of offering in the Celtic language, and then you kill the goat. It is a good sacrifice and will ensure we have a bountiful harvest next year."

Blaze thought about how upset Lillith had been when she'd heard that an animal was sacrificed on Samhain. Now, he didn't want to do it. Sure, it was no different than hunting or slaughtering the livestock to eat over the winter. But after seeing the horror in Lillith's eyes, this all seemed wrong.

"Nay. I won't do it," he said, surprising his mother.

"Blaze, stop fighting who you are and partake of our traditions."

"Mother, I grew up being more like father than you. I never considered myself a warlock and I still don't."

"Is that why you burned my Tarot cards?" She glared at him. "Don't think I don't know what you did."

"Your readings were only upsetting Lillith. There is no need for that."

"This isn't about Lillith, is it? You are still angry at me for leaving for five years and not contacting you. I only did it for you, Blaze. I felt it was better for you if I just disappeared for a while until things calmed down."

"What difference does it make? You're back and nothing is calm anymore."

"Lord Blaze. Lady Minerva," came the voice from one of men from the coven. The coven was made up of both men and women. These were people who lived in secret, either making their homes in the woods or living at a surrounding castle or village, but under false pretense.

"What is it?" asked Minerva.

"We found some intruders," said one of the women, as several of them brought forth Lillith, Orvyn, and Milo.

"God's eyes, nay! Can this night get any worse?" growled Blaze. "Lillith, what the hell are you doing here?"

"I was curious about the Samhain rituals, so I followed you and your mother here," said Lillith.

"And we followed to protect her," said Milo.

Blaze saw the witches holding their weapons, leaving them defenseless. He shook his head. "And we see how well that work out, don't we?" he asked sarcastically.

"Blaze, is that your dagger?" Minerva reached out and took the blade from the coven member.

"Yes. It seems so," said Blaze, taking it from her. "Which one of you stole it from my chamber?"

"It was me," Lillith said too quickly. He had the feeling there was more to this and that she was covering for someone, but he would have to ask her about it later.

"Mother, I'll take them back to the manor," said Blaze.

"It is almost midnight," said one of the witches.

"Yes," agreed Minerva. "There is no time for that, Blaze. They'll just have to wait until we've finished giving thanks to the earth and making our sacrifice. Time is a crucial element if we want to expect a good harvest next year. Go ahead, Blaze."

"Sacrifice?" Lillith's eyes flashed over to the bleating goat and then back to Blaze again. "Nay. Please don't kill the goat, Blaze."

"It is part of our ritual. Now sit down and be quiet, all of you," said Minerva.

"Blaze, please. Don't do it." Lillith looked terrified. Not only of Samhain and witches and the night in general, but also of him. He didn't ever want to do something that would make her afraid of him. It would haunt him for the rest of his life if he did.

"Mother, tonight, we'll make an offering of fruit, grain, and vegetables instead." Blaze waved his hand through the air, looking over at the man holding the goat. "Get that goat out of there and bring some of the baskets filled with our harvest from this year," said Blaze.

"You really shouldn't go changing tradition," warned his mother.

"On the contrary, I like change," said Blaze, handing his dagger to his mother. "By the way, I don't want this anymore, so you can keep it."

"I don't want it," said Minerva.

"I'll take it," said Orvyn, surprising Blaze.

"You?" asked Blaze. "Whatever for?"

"I suppose this is as good of a time as any to let you know my secret."

"Which secret is that?" asked Blaze, thinking the man was going to tell him why he'd been meeting with the villagers in secret and exchanging missives.

"My late wife used to be a witch," said Orvyn.

"What?" gasped Lillith.

"Who was your wife?" Minerva wanted to know.

"Her name was Daisy. She was a cook for the Earl of Birmingham where I used to be kennel groom. That's where I met her."

"I know her. She was part of our coven," said Minerva. "She was a fine woman. When did she die?"

"Four years ago, my lady."

"I'm sorry," said Minerva.

Blaze cleared his throat. "So, Orvyn. You mean to tell me you've kept a secret as big as this? I didn't think it was possible."

"Well, as Lady Lillith says, sometimes people are not what they seem," Orvyn told him. "There is something else I need to tell you as well, my lord."

"Lady Minerva, the moon is full and it is midnight," said one of the coven members.

"It'll have to wait," said Blaze. "Go ahead and start the ceremony, Mother."

"Will your dead wife be coming back tonight as well, Orvyn?" Milo whispered.

Blaze glanced over his shoulder at the boy. He was the only loose end now. If he opened his mouth and told everyone what he saw here tonight, it could ruin Blaze forever.

Lillith was excited to be witnessing the ritual of Samhain, yet she felt a little frightened too. She wasn't sure what to expect, especially when it came to summoning the dead. That is, if that was what these people did.

"Lillith, I don't have to stay." Blaze took her arm. "Why don't I take you and the others back to the manor?"

"Nay. I want to stay," said Milo, overhearing him.

"Me too," agreed Orvyn. "My wife never let me attend one of your bonfires and I am curious as to what happens."

"None of you are scared?" asked Blaze.

The men shook their heads.

"I'm not frightened as long as I'm with you, Blaze," said Lillith.

"I have to have a promise from each of you that you are not going to say a word about this to anyone once we get back to the manor."

They all agreed

"Milo, if you say one word about this to anyone, I swear I'll have a curse put on you," warned Blaze.

The boy's eyes opened wide in fright. "I won't," he promised.

"Blaze, stop scaring the boy," scolded Lillith in a low voice behind her hand so Milo wouldn't hear her. "You don't really know how to curse people. Do you?"

"Nay," he said flippantly. "I just wanted to stress how serious this situation was. Sometimes a little fear goes a long way."

"He's not going to hurt you, Milo," Lillith told the pageboy. "No one will. But please, for all or our sakes, you need to keep quiet about this."

"I understand." Milo looked down and stared at the ground, no longer even able to look directly at Blaze, probably thinking direct eye contact might curse him.

"Do you think he'll keep the secret?" asked Blaze softly.

Lillith wasn't sure Milo would keep this a secret, but they had no choice but to trust that he would. "I'll talk to him more once we return to the manor."

"It's time, Minerva," said one of the men who was wearing a mask that looked like a deer. It was made of fur and had antlers attached to the top.

"Say the incantation and make the offering," said a woman dressed like a bird. Her headdress had feathers sticking out in all directions.

"Blaze, it's up to you this year." Minerva handed him back his dagger and donned her mask. "Put your mask on."

"I will not," said Blaze.

"Blaze, we made it specially for you. I'm going to wear mine," said Lillith, pulling it out of her bag and tying it around her head.

Blaze let out a whoosh of air from his mouth and dug the mask out of his pocket. "I never could tell you no, Lilly." He put the mask on.

Lillith saw the goat tied to a tree and ran over and gathered it into her arms. "Please, not the goat, Blaze." Orvyn and Milo walked over and sat down next to her on the ground.

"I am changing tradition just for you, Lillith." Blaze took his blade and walked over to a basket of fruit, stabbing an apple with the point of his dagger. Then he took an armful of wheat and a lit torch and brought them over to the flat rock that was next to the bonfire.

Minerva started chanting in a different language.

"I wonder what she's saying?" asked Milo in a whisper.

"She's speaking Gaelic," Orvyn whispered back. "She is thanking the earth for the gifts and praying for a prosperous harvest next year."

"You know the language?" asked Lillith.

"My wife spoke Gaelic and I learned it too," he told her.

"I still don't understand what this is all about," said Milo.

"Samhain recognizes the end of the harvest season and the beginning of the dark times – or winter," explained Orvyn. "The witches are in tune with the land and worship everything of the earth. They believe the earth is alive. By doing this ritual, they are giving thanks for all they have and asking for a blessing for a bountiful harvest starting with the growth of new life in the spring."

"There doesn't seem anything wrong with that," said Lillith with a nod of her head.

"There isn't," agreed Orvyn, smiling, looking happy to be there.

"But they're still witches," said Milo. "Surely, there is something wrong with that."

"Nay. I don't believe so," Lillith answered, still hugging the goat and rubbing her hand over its ears. "What I learned from Blaze and Minerva is that people often think the worst of them and that is why they need to keep who and what they are a secret."

"So, they don't practice dark magic and curse and kill people?" asked Milo.

"Not them," said Lillith. "Although, I can't say that is true for all witches."

"Then witches and warlocks aren't evil and dark and nasty?" asked Milo, still trying to understand things.

"Some of them can be," Blaze interrupted, suddenly standing right behind them. Lillith hadn't even known he was there. "However, my mother and her coven, as well as me are not that way at all."

"But . . . c-could any of you curse someone if you wanted to?"

Blaze chuckled and ruffled the boy's hair with his hand. "No one cursed and killed Lillith's brother, Robert, and neither will I or anyone curse you, if that is what you are worried about."

"If you ask me, people curse themselves with their opinions, judgements, and beliefs," said Lillith, starting to understand this all easily now.

"That's right, Lilly Bee," said Blaze, flashing her a smile, causing her heart to melt.

"What's next?" asked Lillith.

"There is a prayer for the dead and then everyone dances around the fire," explained Blaze.

"Is this when the spirits arrive?" asked Milo, sounding curious but scared. "The dead that come from another world to walk the earth? I'm not sure I want to see this after all."

"We don't need to stay for this part. I'll take you all back now," said Blaze. "Get your horses. I'll tell my mother I'll come back for her later. I'll be right with you."

Orvyn and Milo went to the horses and Blaze walked away to speak to his mother.

"Well, you live another day thanks to me, little goat." Lillith gave the goat a kiss on the head and turned to collect her horse. She stopped dead in her tracks when she thought she heard her father's voice from behind her.

"Liiiiiilllllllith," she heard a deep, low whisper.

Lillith shook her head, thinking it was her imagination. After all, there was music and chanting and lots of noise coming from around the bonfire. They'd been burning herbs since she arrived, and Lillith actually felt a little dizzy. She figured she was only imagining it all.

"Liiiiilllllith," she heard her father's voice again. Slowly turning, she faced the fire, squinting to see the image of a man rising up from the smoke.

"F-Father?" she asked in a half whisper. "Is that you?"

"It is," she heard him say, not sure if the voice was only in her mind.

"Is Robert with you?"

"Nay. Why would he be?" her father snorted. She walked closer to the bonfire, keeping her focus on the image of the see-through man, not even seeing anyone else. Part of her was excited that her father was here. Another part of her was terrified.

"Father? I'm sorry I didn't have a chance to say goodbye to you."

"I'm sssssssorry," she heard, straining her ears since his image as well as his voice was getting fainter.

"Sorry for what?" she asked. "Oh, you mean the feud."

"And your . . . beeeetrothal."

"Oh, Father, I love Blaze. I don't want to marry the baron. But Uncle Arthur insists I have to."

"My brooooother is a fool."

"I wish you were here to help me."

"I will aaaaaalways beeeee . . . with you . . . Liiiiiillllith."

"Wait, don't leave," she said, as his image started to fade. "I have so much more to say. To ask you."

"Lilly?" Blaze's hand on her shoulder made her whirl around. "Who are you talking to?"

"It's my father, Blaze. There, in the bonfire. Look." She pointed to the fire, but the image of her father was gone.

"It's been a long day, sweetheart, and I'm sure the burning herbs are making you heady. Let's get you home." He put his arm around her and headed toward the horses.

"You believe me, don't you? I mean, I never thought I'd see a spirit in the fire, but I did. My father even spoke to me. He said he was sorry for the feud and that his brother was a fool."

Blaze chuckled. "Well, that's about right, I guess. However, I didn't see any spirits. I think you're overtired. Here, have a drink." He handed her a flask made from deerskin.

"What is this?" she asked, peering into the cup. The strong aroma assaulted her nostrils, though the scent was more alluring than repulsive.

"Some things are better not to ask," said Blaze with a grin.

"All right," she said, drinking of the liquid, relaxing immediately. "Mmmm," she said. "Not bad. It tastes like some kind of herbal wine."

"My guess is exactly that."

She took another big swig, gulping it down greedily.

"That's enough," he said, taking the wineskin away from her. "I have a feeling you will sleep well tonight."

With his arm around her, Lillith leaned in to him, liking the warmth that was being shared between them. It felt so right to be with Blaze. There was no doubt in her mind that they belonged together.

"Aye," she agreed, looking up and smiling. "I think I will have sweet dreams tonight. Thank you, Blaze."

Eighteen

BLAZE HAD SLEPT SOUNDLY, but was rudely awoken the next morning by a pounding on his solar door.

"What is it? I'm trying to sleep," he ground out.

The door opened and Emery stuck his head inside. "I'm sorry to bother you so early, my lord, but it seems visitors have arrived, unannounced."

"Well, send them away." He rolled on to his side, wanting to go back to sleep since he'd been dreaming about making love with Lillith.

Emery cleared his throat and didn't leave.

"Well? What is it? If you have something else to say, then speak."

"Blaze, get up. Quickly," said Lilly, running past Emery into the room, still tying her bodice of her purple gown.

"What the hell? Can't a man get some sleep around here?" He yawned and sat up in bed, stretching. He slept in the nude, and saw Lillith's mouth and eyes open wide when she noticed. He looked down to see that the sheet was not covering him, and his dreams of Lilly had giving him an erection.

"Oh!" gasped Lillith, covering her eyes with her hand.

"God's teeth, what is going on?" He grabbed his trews and pulled them on, standing up and continuing to dress.

"You'll never believe who is here," said Emery.

"I'm sure one of you is about to tell me."

"Uncle Arthur and my mother have arrived, and Arthur is insisting your wedding with Serena will happen now. Immediately," said Lillith.

"What?" That woke him up. "He can't do that. It's too soon and the banns have not even been posted."

"Actually, he can my lord." Emery pulled a rolled-up parchment out from under his arm. "It seems the final agreement you signed . . . before reading it . . . says the wedding will take place when and where Arthur decides."

"God's eyes, can this get any worse? Why in hell is he doing this?" Blaze continued to dress.

"Someone else has arrived as well," said Lillith, lowering her hand and wringing them both together.

"Nothing could be worse. Who is it?" Blaze finished dressing and buckled his weapon belt around him.

"He brought the Earl of Birmingham with him, my lord," Emery answered.

"What?" Blaze's hands stilled, and his heart almost stopped. He hoped he had heard Emery wrong. "Whatever for?"

"I'm not sure, my lord, but I think it has something to do with your request for knighthood."

"He's here personally to give me his answer. It must be a good thing," said Blaze excitedly, brushing past Lillith and heading out the door.

They all made their way to the great hall where their visitors were awaiting them.

"My lords," said Blaze with a nod and a bow, acknowledging both the earl and Lord Arthur.

"Lillith," said Beatrice, hugging her daughter.

"Mother," came Serena's voice from behind him. Serena walked up on her own, holding on to Posy's arm.

"You're walking by yourself?" asked Lillith.

"Yes, isn't it wonderful? Lady Minerva's potion seemed to heal my swollen ankle quickly." Serena looked at her foot, inspecting it from all positions.

"Potion?" asked the earl suspiciously. "What kind of potion?"

Serena's eyes flashed over to Lillith's, and Blaze held his breath. He hoped the word witch wasn't going to be mentioned.

"Natural herbs used by healers. Naught else," Lillith answered for her.

"Yes, that's right," said Serena. Thankfully, Posy didn't say a word.

"What are you doing here, Lord Arthur?" asked the earl.

"I'm here for my niece's wedding to Lord Blaze," Arthur answered. "I brought a priest with us who will marry Beatrice and me as well."

"A double wedding. How nice," said the earl. "So, you'll be aligned with the Paynes then?"

"Yes. We will," said Arthur.

Blaze saw Milo and Orvyn enter the great hall and head in their direction. This was the last thing he needed right now. If either one of them said a word about what they saw last night, Blaze would have no chance of knighthood, marriage or anything else. He'd be lucky not to be burned at the stake along with his mother.

"Before the wedding takes place, I have something to discuss with Lord Payne, regarding his request for knighthood," said the earl.

"My lord, I had no idea you were coming. Have you made a decision, then?" asked Blaze, feeling as nervous as he was the first time he kissed Lillith.

"As you know, Lord Blaze, your father was once my head knight and one of my most trusted men," said the earl. "However, you were only training to be a knight."

"Yes. Of course," Blaze answered. "I have completed the rest of the training on my own over the past five years. I have practiced and kept up with my skills and am ready now," Blaze said, trying to convince the earl.

"Aye, I agree you are more than ready," said the earl. "However, there is one thing I needed to know before I give you an answer."

"Of course. What is it you need to know? I'll tell you anything," said Blaze.

"My question isn't for you, Blaze. It is for my spy that I've put here, watching you for the last year."

"Spy?" Blaze didn't like the sound of this.

"Yes. My man tells me your skills are exceptional, but I haven't heard an answer from him on my other question, so I decided to just show up and ask him myself."

"I'm sorry," said Blaze. "I don't understand."

"I can explain." Orvyn stepped up to join them.

"Orvyn? You're the earl's spy?" asked Blaze. This was the last thing he ever expected to hear.

"I've always been able to trust Orvyn completely, plus he is my cousin," said the earl. "That's why I planted him here at Skull Manor to watch you and report back to me."

"This has something to do with you meeting with villagers in secret?" asked Blaze.

"Aye," said Orvyn. "It was our way of staying in touch. The earl sent missives to a certain villager he trusts, and we used him to send messages back and forth so you wouldn't become suspicious. He sent a missive last night, but you stopped me from going to the village and I was not able to respond."

"What is this all for?" grumbled Blaze, crossing his arms over his chest, not liking to be fooled.

"I needed to know for sure if the rumors of your family being witches was true or not," stated the earl, making Blaze cringe. This was it. The time of reckoning. Orvyn could expose them all, or he could help put the rumors to rest.

"And you asked Orvyn to find out." Blaze glanced over at

Orvyn who looked just as nervous as Blaze felt. He hoped he could count on the man to help him. He hoped that after what he'd found out last night, that the man could be trusted. After all, exposing Blake and his mother would only be exposing his dead wife as well. That would break any trust between the cousins.

"Orvyn, tell me," said the earl, right in front of everyone. "Have you seen any evidence of this family, especially Lord Blaze, doing anything at all that would be considered . . . witchy?"

There wasn't a sound in the room as they all waited for Orvyn's answer. Everything depended on what he would say.

"Nay, Earl Birmingham, I can't say I saw anything witchy at all for the entire time I've been here. As a matter of fact, the Payne family is just as normal as anyone else. I'm afraid everything bad you've heard was nothing but just rumors."

"See? I told you so," spat Arthur. "Now, let's get on with our double wedding."

"Wait, just a minute." The earl rubbed his chin in thought. "Has anyone else seen or heard anything that would make them think this family were witches?"

Blaze's eyes shot over to Milo. The pageboy's eyes interlocked with his. If Blaze could probe minds, he'd put the curse idea back into the boy's mind again, just to scare him and keep him from running at the mouth.

"No one?" the earl asked again. Blaze looked over to the hand-maid Posy now. She was staring at the ground. "Well, then, it's settled. Lord Blaze, please step forward." The earl drew his blade.

"Of course, my lord." Blaze walked over to the earl.

"Down on one knee, Payne," commanded the earl. Blaze did as told. The earl said a few words and then tapped each of Blaze's shoulders with his sword. "I dub you, Sir Blaze Payne. Now get up, and go marry your bride, Sir Blaze. We are all waiting."

"Thank you," said Blaze, feeling so happy to finally be a knight. It was what he'd always wanted. He turned with a smile on his face, but stopped when he saw Lillith, looking as if she were about to cry. He couldn't go through with this after all. He wouldn't do this to Lillith. He had no choice but to contest the betrothal and refuse to marry Serena.

He was about to speak up, when two men entered the great hall accompanied by his mother.

Lillith turned and ran, not wanting to have to watch Blaze marry her sister. But through her tears, she couldn't see where she was going, and knocked into someone entering the great hall.

"Oh, I'm sorry," she apologized to the man. "I should have watched where I was going."

"Lillith?" asked the man. She looked up to see her betrothed, the baron. "I didn't have to go to France after all, so we can get married earlier than expected."

"Edward!" she exclaimed, her eyes darting back to Blaze. Then the second man stepped forward and her mouth dropped open when she realized it was her brother, Robert.

"Hello, Lillith," said Robert, smiling and holding out his arms.

"Robert!" Lillith dove into his arms for a hug, burying her face against his chest, crying. She was not able to believe it was really him.

"Robert? My son?" Beatrice put a hand to her mouth.

"Brother? You're alive?" squealed Serena. She grabbed her mother's hand and they ran to greet him.

"What is this?" spat Arthur.

"It seems Robert Bonnel wasn't cursed and killed by witches after all," said Blaze.

"Of course not," said Robert with a chuckle. "Why would anyone think that? I've been traveling to the holy lands, doing work for the king for the past five years in secret. I'm sorry I couldn't tell anyone, but now I'm finished."

"Oh, Robert, I am so glad you are alive," said Lillith as her brother laughed and hugged all three women.

"I don't understand," said Beatrice. "Your father and I heard from eye witnesses that you were atop a cliff mumbling nonsense and then you jumped to your death into the sea."

"What?" Robert chuckled. "I often went up to the cliffs and talked to myself, since I couldn't tell anyone the king's secret business – which I still can't say a word about by the way. But why would someone think I jumped to my death?"

"Your hat was found floating in the sea," said Serena.

"Ah, yes. The wind blew it off and I must admit I cursed a little and climbed down the cliff to look for it but never found it. I'm sorry to have worried you all. I wish I could have told you, but the king swore me to secrecy."

"He never should have worried your family this way," agreed Blaze.

"King Edward is odd at times, but you didn't hear that from me," said the earl.

"Where's Father?" Robert smiled, looking around the room. "I want to tell him about all the lands I saw."

"Oh, Robert," said his mother, taking his hands and crying.

"Father died a week ago," said Lillith. "He went out riding, drunk, and fell on his own blade."

"Nay," said Robert, his smile disappearing. "That's horrible. I'm so sorry I wasn't here."

"You're here now, and that is all that matters," said Lillith.

"I am." Robert still hugged his family. "And I will carry on in Father's stead. I will be the Lord of Alderwood Castle, since I am his only heir."

"Does that mean Mother won't have to marry Uncle Arthur?" asked Serena.

"Nay, of course not," said Robert with a chuckle. "Why would she?" He gave his mother a kiss. "Mother, you don't ever have to marry again if you choose not to. I'll never throw you out."

Lillith looked over to see Arthur sinking atop a chair, looking like he was devastated. However, Lillith felt so happy that she didn't care what happened to the vile man.

"Well, shall we continue with your sisters' weddings?" asked the earl. "I will stay for the wedding feast, but need to leave right afterwards."

"Yes," said the baron, Sir Edward, taking Lillith's hand. "I cannot wait to marry this wonderful woman."

"I'm ready," said the priest, standing up at the dais. "Will the two couples please approach the dais?"

Lillith didn't know what to do. Feeling as if her world had come to an end, she accompanied the baron up to the dais, where Blaze and Serena were already waiting.

"Wait a minute," said Blaze with his hand in the air.

"Is there a problem, Sir Blaze?" asked the earl.

"Yes, I'm afraid there is, Earl Birmingham," Blaze answered. "It seems I have been tricked into agreeing to marry the wrong Lady Bonnel."

"Blaze, please," whispered Lillith, knowing this could only cause trouble.

"What do you mean?" asked the earl. "You'd better explain, Payne."

The crowd all mumbled softly, watching from afar.

"When I agreed to marry Lady Bonnel and end the feud, I thought I was marrying my childhood sweetheart and the love of my life, Lillith," said Blaze.

Lillith bit her lip and looked to the ground.

"Go on," said the earl.

"Lord Arthur purposely wrote up the proposal omitting the first name of which girl I was to marry," Blaze continued. "I, of course, was sure it was Lillith, since we have had a verbal agreement with Lord Henri Bonnel since childhood that we'd marry someday."

"Is this true, Lord Arthur?" asked the earl.

Arthur had been trying to silently sneak out of the great hall, but Minerva stood in his way, blocking him from leaving.

"Well, I can't be sure," said Arthur.

"I can," said Minerva. "I'm Blaze's mother and I can tell you that my son and Lady Lillith were inseparable when they were growing up."

"That's right," agreed Beatrice. "My husband did have a verbal agreement with Roger. However, when Robert disappeared and the rumors started that he was cursed and killed by Lady Minerva because she was a witch, the feud started between our families and everything changed."

"Feud?" asked Robert. "I think I've been gone longer than I thought. It seems I've missed a lot, and also caused a lot of trouble."

"I'm confused," said the earl. "If you two were promised to each other and both your fathers are dead, then why is Sir Blaze marrying the wrong sister?"

"I can answer that," said the baron. "It is because Lord Henri Bonnel came to me with a betrothal just before he died. He offered me Lady Lillith's hand in marriage, and I accepted. However, I didn't know about the verbal betrothal that happened long ago. If I had, of course, I would never have accepted the proposal."

"Really?" Lillith looked up, feeling hope for the first time in years. "Then, will you let us break the betrothal, so Blaze and I can marry?"

"Well, I wouldn't mind, but it seems it's too late," said the baron. "Blaze is already betrothed to Serena. Am I right?"

"Under false pretense," said Blaze.

"Serena's name is written on the document and signed by Lord Payne," said Arthur. "It's not my fault if he blindly signs things he doesn't read first. They still need to get married. I refuse to break the contract."

"Now, wait a minute, Uncle." Robert walked to the front of the room. "You no longer have a say in this. I am my father's heir and also Lord of Alderwood Castle now. And I say, if the baron agrees, then the betrothal can be broken so my sister Lillith and Sir Blaze can marry."

"Oh, thank you, Robert!" Lillith ran to her brother and hugged him. But when she looked over to Serena and saw how sad she looked, she knew this wasn't right. "Nay. I can't do it," she said, standing up straight. "It wouldn't be right."

"What did you say, Lilly?" Blaze rushed over. "It's all taken care of. Now we can get married. Why are you changing your mind?"

"I'm sorry, Blaze. It breaks my heart to say this, but it's not fair to Serena," said Lillith. "She wants to get married just as much as I do. Plus, I know she's grown fond of you, Blaze."

"Nay, Sister, it's fine," said Serena, wiping tears from her eyes. "I know how in love you two are. I don't want to stand between you." Her mother put her arm around her to comfort her.

"I have a solution," said Edward.

"What is it, Baron?" asked the earl.

"Let me marry the lovely, Lady Serena." He bowed and took Serena's hand and kissed it.

"Really? You want to marry me?" asked Serena through her tears.

"I have had the pleasure of visiting and getting to know both the Ladies Bonnel lately, and I must say that each is just as charming. I would be honored to marry either one of them."

"Oh, Serena, what do you say?" asked Lillith, holding her breath, hoping Serena would agree to marry the baron.

"I would be honored to marry you, Baron Bancroft." Serena stopped crying and started smiling as she curtsied to the man.

The priest cleared his throat. "Will there still be a wedding or not, my lords?"

"Nay. There will be two weddings," said Blaze, taking Lillith's hand and leading her over to the priest. Serena couldn't stop smiling as she stood next to Lillith taking her hand and standing next to Baron Edward Bancroft.

"Oh, Sister, We're both getting married," Serena whispered to Lillith. "This is a dream come true."

The ceremony was quick and simple, and before Lillith realized it, she was Blaze's wife.

"Since I didn't know I'd be getting married today, I don't have a ring for you yet, Lilly," Blaze told her.

"I have this one for now." Lillith held up the toy ring from the cake that she was still wearing.

"Let me kiss you, my wife," said Blaze, taking her into his arms and kissing her deeply. Then he looked out to everyone in the great hall and made an announcement. "There will be a grand wedding feast to celebrate the double weddings today and everyone is invited."

Cheers went up and the musicians started playing music while the servants hurried around to prepare a feast.

"I can't believe it," Blaze said, still hugging Lillith. "Everything worked out. Who would have even guessed this could happen?"

"It was in the cards," said Minerva, congratulating them both with hugs.

"The cards?" asked Lillith. "But I had a horrible reading," she whispered.

"The death card meant the death of an old betrothal, and the other cards showed the start of a new one," she explained.

"And that fool card was me, going on a journey," chuckled Blaze. "I'm just happy how it ended."

"My father knew this would happen," said Lillith. "He knew and he told me from the grave last night."

"I believe you," said Blaze, kissing her on the nose. "But let's not talk about that anymore until the earl and baron leaves, shall we?"

"Congratulations, Lord and Lady Payne. Orvyn walked up with Milo. Orvyn was smiling from ear to ear as he shook Blaze's hand.

"Earl Birmingham," Blaze called out. "Can I steal Orvyn from you? I need a good stablemaster, and he has been more than I could ever ask for."

"It's fine with me, Payne, the earl called back, busy drinking wine and talking with Robert.

"Thank you, Lord Payne," said Orvyn. "Skull Manor is where I belong."

"I believe that's true," said Blaze.

"Milo, I'll miss you," said Lillith, giving the boy a hug. He looked so forlorn.

"Have you enjoyed your stay at Skull Manor, Milo?" asked Blaze.

"Yes, my lord," said Milo, still not looking directly at them.

"You know, now that I'm a knight I'm going to be looking for other knights to live at the manor. That means, I'll also need to train some boys to someday be squires. Would you care to stay on at the manor and train under me personally?"

Milo's head snapped up with a jerk. "Really? Train to be a squire? Really, Sir?" asked Milo.

"I'm not saying it'll happen right away, and I can't guarantee which knight you'd be a squire for, but that would all depend on how fast you learn."

"I'll do it!" said Milo. "Yes! I don't care how long it takes, but I want to be a squire more than anything else."

"Then, as long as Lord Robert doesn't mind, you'll be in my care from now on."

"I can speak for Robert and tell you my brother won't mind at all," said Lillith. "Welcome to Skull Manor, Milo."

"Thank you, my lord and lady. Thank you so much." Milo bowed about ten times and then ran off in excitement.

"That was nice of you," said Lillith to her new husband.

"Well, I knew how much he wanted it, since I felt the same way about being knighted. Besides, what better way to keep a close eye on him so he doesn't run at the mouth, if you know what I mean."

"Blaze, I have never been happier," said Lillith, standing on her tiptoes to kiss him. He picked her up in his arms and kissed her passionately.

"Well, wife, I'm willing to bet that after our wedding night you'll be feeling even happier. I know I will. I have waited such a long time for this. It is like a dream come true."

Minerva picked up her cat in her arms, now talking with Lillith's mother.

"It is nice not to be feuding anymore," said Beatrice.

"I'm looking forward to getting to know you better now that we are related through marriage," said Minerva.

"I'd like that. And you'll have to tell me who makes your gown. It is stunning," gushed Beatrice.

"I can have one made for you, if you'd like." Minerva looked over at Blaze and Lillith and winked.

"I would love it," answered Beatrice. "And make sure it has plenty of those little moons and stars on it. I really admire them."

"Oh no," said Blaze softly. "Lilly, before you know it, your mother is going to be doing things she's never done before."

"Mother, come talk with me and my new husband." Serena pulled her mother away, leaving just Minerva with Blaze and Lillith.

"Mother, you're not really going to make a gown like that for her, are you?" Blaze put Lillith down.

"Of course, I am. If things go well, I might be making them for the entire castle."

Blaze groaned and Lillith laughed.

"Tell me, why did you walk in with Lillith's brother and betrothed?" asked Blaze. "Where did you even find them?"

"I had a vision last night from Lillith's father too," whispered Minerva. "He told me where to find them. Even though, if I would have had my cards, I might have been able to find out for myself."

"So, where were they?" asked Lillith. "My brother and the baron."

"It's the oddest thing," said Minerva. "They were both stalled on the road. Robert's horse went lame, and the baron's wagon lost a wheel. I found them and just directed them back here."

"It was Father," whispered Lillith. "I know it was him. He helped me, just like I knew he would."

"So, do you believe in our ways now, my daughter-by-marriage?" asked Minerva.

"I must say, I'm starting to think that I feared something only because I knew nothing about it," Lillith told her. "But I know more now. I'm changing and more than willing to learn everything I can."

"And I can't wait to teach you," Minerva answered.

"Me too," said Blaze, giving her a sultry look, speaking about something different entirely.

Blaze's raven flew in an open window and swooped down over their heads, scaring the cat. Sam bounded out of Minerva's arms and jumped onto the trestle table, running from the bird.

"I'd better go take care of this. Excuse me," said Minerva, leaving.

"Blaze. I mean, Husband," said Lillith, as Blaze kissed her head and then her neck, not caring who was watching.

"What is it, Lilly Bee? Did you want me to stop?"

"Stop? Nay. Never," she said with a giggle. "I was just wondering. Don't you think it is odd that with all we went through that we'd end up together, happy and married? I really think my father had something to do with this from the grave."

"Mayhap," he said, still kissing her. "But what does it matter? We're together, married, and I'm a knight. And the best part is that we will no longer be two lost souls searching for what we thought we would never have."

"True," said Lillith. "But I still feel a little odd. Like even though my father helped us, I don't want to be haunted by a spirit."

"You won't," he told her. "Lilly, all that stuff about ghosts and being haunted is really just stories to scare people I think. None of it can actually hurt us."

"You're right," she answered, feeling the weight of the world off her shoulders now. "No longer will we have to live like strangers in the night. Now, we will wake up every morning in love in each other's arms."

"That's right," agreed Blaze. "We can finally put behind all our trials, tribulations, and especially our ***Haunted Hearts***."

From the Author

I hope you enjoyed Blaze and Lillith's story and will take a moment to leave a review for me.

Although the use of Tarot cards wasn't really happening yet at this time, there were still witches and gypsies reading fortunes from cards from way back. Usually, it was with a normal deck of cards. The ones that had pictures on them were not the same as the Tarot as we know it, but the pictures changed through the years. Therefore, that is one of the reasons I didn't refer to the cards as the Tarot, even though, in my mind, that is what Minerva was using.

Samhain (pronounced Sahw-in) was an ancient Celtic or Druid tradition of giving thanks to the land at the end of the harvest season and praying for a good crop for the following year. It was a time that marked their new year. It was after the harvest but before the approaching winter, which they associated with death. A bonfire usually accompanied this ritual, and it was thought that the veil between the living and spirit world was the thinnest at this time. They honored their dead ancestors, and it was said that on this night, the dead could walk the earth once more.

Soul cakes, small hand-sized buns filled with spices and a cross of currants on top, were given out to the beggars and children in exchange for a prayer for a dead loved one. There were no pumpkins in medieval England. They used turnips which they hollowed out and carved a spooky face into, lighting them up with a candle inside. They were placed on doorsteps and windowsills on Samhain, used to ward away evil spirits. Costumes were also worn for protection, trying to confuse evil spirits that might walk the earth that night.

The Catholic church, trying to convert as many people as

possible, moved All Saints Day and All Souls Day, which was once in May, to the beginning of November, to coincide with Samhain. They called it All Hallows' Day instead. It was their version of the pagan tradition of Samhain.

So, you see that a lot of these traditions, many years later, filtered through into the holiday of Hallowe'en – a contraction for Hallows' Evening. Or Halloween, as we know it. Children still carve jack-o-lanterns and dress up going begging from door to door – trick-or-treating.

Things change through time, but in another way, it really all stays the same.

If you're interested in another ancient Celtic festival called Beltane, which is May Day as we know it, please read *May Queen* – Book 5 of my Holiday Knights Series. Each of the books in this series incorporates the roots of some of our favorite holidays and shows how they originated way back when. Some of the other holidays I explore in the series are Valentine's Day, New Years, Easter, and of course, Christmas.

Thank you,

Elizabeth Rose

About Elizabeth

Elizabeth Rose is a multi-published, bestselling, award-winning author with over 100 books. She writes medieval, historical, contemporary, paranormal, and western romance. Her books are available as Ebooks, paperback, and audiobooks as well.

Her favorite characters in her works include dark, dangerous and tortured heroes, and feisty, independent heroines who know how to wield a sword. She loves writing 14th century medieval novels, and is well-known for her many series.

Elizabeth is a born storyteller and passionate about sharing her works with her readers. In the summertime you can find her in her writing hammock in her secret garden, creating her next novel.

Please be sure to visit her website at **Elizabethrosenovels.com** to read excerpts from any of her novels and get sneak peeks at covers of upcoming books. Be sure to sign up for her **newsletter** so you don't miss out on new releases or upcoming events.

Also by Elizabeth Rose

Romantic Fantasy Series

Portals of Destiny

Medieval Series

Legendary Bastards of the Crown Series

Seasons of Fortitude Series

Secrets of the Heart Series

Legacy of the Blade Series

Daughters of the Dagger Series

MadMan MacKeefe Series

Barons of the Cinque Ports Series

Holiday Knights Series

Highland Chronicles Series

Pirate Lords Series

Highland Outcasts

Medieval/Paranormal Series

Elemental Magick Series

Greek Myth Fantasy Series

Tangled Tales Series

Contemporary Series

Tarnished Saints Series

Working Man Series

Western Series

Cowboys of the Old West Series

And More!

Please visit http://elizabethrosenovels.com